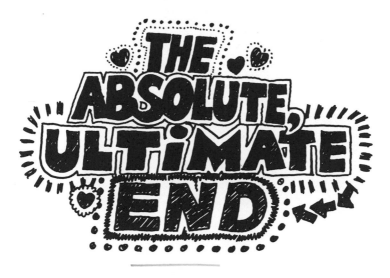

THE ABSOLUTE, ULTIMATE END

A Novel by Julia First

FRANKLIN WATTS
NEW YORK   LONDON   TORONTO   SYDNEY
1985

Sincere appreciation to
Rosemary Sheehan and Carol Macknin
of the Kennedy School
in Medford, Massachusetts;
to Bill Jesdale of Meadowbrook and
to Stan Kress, somewhere in Idaho.

Library of Congress Cataloging in Publication Data

First, Julia.
The absolute, ultimate end.

Summary: Eighth-grader Maggie's new friendship
with a blind girl leads her to fear for the continuation
of the school's program for the handicapped when
the school board threatens major cutbacks.
[1. Schools—Fiction. 2. Blind—Fiction.
3. Physically handicapped—Fiction] I. Title.
PZ7.F49875Ab 1985   [Fic]   85-9030
ISBN 0-531-10075-8

The Absolute, Ultimate End

*To Joshy. Enos I think
he's a First-rate Feller.*

Chapter One

I'll be honest with you. I went bonkers the minute I saw him.

It was last year, the first week of seventh grade that I met Stevie. Well, I didn't exactly *meet* him in the sense of getting a formal introduction. . . . I noticed his presence was it. But actually, that was all I needed.

It was sign-up day for all extracurricular activities, and my friend Eloise and I were in the gym where thousands of bodies were milling around tables with huge signs. Everyone was shoving and elbowing, but of course seventh graders got pushed more than they shoved, and we were pretty bewildered by the whole scene.

"Do you think I could make the team, Maggie?" Eloise asked me as we passed the table marked Baseball.

"Well, natch," I told her. Ordinarily, Eloise doesn't need any reassurance in that area. I mean, she is a female jock. She had to be the only kid on the block of either sex who made the Little League on her first try. But when you're starting junior high, it takes some getting used to before you dare expose your real personality.

So she was a little nervous at the beginning and sort of scrawled her name on the tryout list, half hoping it wouldn't be legible. But by the time we'd passed Basketball, Soccer, and Field Hockey, she'd gotten her confidence back and wrote her name at all the tables so there'd be no question the letters spelled out Eloise Barton, seventh grade.

"Now what about you, Mag?"

"I don't know." I shrugged. "Nothing so far has hit me."

I'm no athlete, or even a sports fan. Up until then my only special interest was geography. And that's only because I've never been more than fifty miles from Oakdale, Massachusetts, where I live. I mean, talk about deprivation, half the people I know have been to Europe. In fact, so many times that to them it's like yawn-yawn. Eloise, too. Her father is a lawyer, and she gets to go with her parents whenever there's a legal convention anywhere. Like Hawaii. She's been there twice and naturally stopped off in San Francisco coming and going, both times!

But anyway, there was no listing of a Geography Club and that day, there we were standing between Gourmet Chefs and School Newspaper, when I looked across the room where a space had opened up, and I flipped. There was this boy, divinely handsome, smiling, and with teeth so white they sparkled across that mammoth room. His hair was dark and thick, and as I watched, he brushed a lock away from his forehead in a way that totally wiped me out.

"Over there." This guttural sound came out of my throat. "I'll sign up over there, whatever it is."

"Where?"

The space was closed up already, and I knew I had to hurry or I'd lose him.

"Follow me," I gurgled and pulled her after me as I pushed and squeezed and made it to the other side before he was gone.

The table was marked Dramatics Club. I squirmed until I stood right behind him and saw him put his name, Steve Garber, and eighth grade, on the paper. Exactly under it, I wrote in my best handwriting, Margaret (Maggie) Thayer, seventh grade. Just seeing our names close like that gave me a thrill.

As he left the table, a boy beside him said, "If you get to play opposite Carrie Dean, Garber, I'll murder you."

"How do you know I'll get a part?" His voice was a real deep dark brown, which showed clearly how mature he was for his age.

The other boy kind of smirked. "Don't be so modest, Garber."

"It's not modesty, Cooper. You have to be good. Maybe Carrie won't get a part either."

"You kidding?" the one whose name was Cooper said. "The way she's put together, she'll get a part all right."

"She'll still have to be able to act," Stevie told him without any kind of a wisecrack in his tone, which was proof to me that this was a totally perfect human being.

He moved out of sight, and I took a very satisfactory breath in anticipation of seeing him again at tryouts. I had no idea of my acting ability, but my motive was strong. And if he thought that being able to act was more important than how a girl was put together, then I had at least a twenty-five percent chance to make it with Stevie Garber. I figured with *his* looks it had to be a cinch he'd get the lead in any play Woodrow Wilson Junior High School would present.

He did. They put on *My Fair Lady*, and I swear every seventh and eighth grade girl competed for the Eliza Doolittle part. Obviously I wasn't the only one who got goose bumps over Stevie. It turned out I didn't get picked for Eliza. But I made the cast with a small three-sentence part. Not opposite Stevie, but at least I saw him at rehearsals and watched him perform. Frankly, even though I think he is a terrific actor, I really didn't think his heart was in the scenes with Carrie, who played Eliza. That was just my personal observation. It certainly wasn't that he was holding back on account of he was afraid his friend Cooper was going to murder him.

Only once did I have a painful doubt. It was during a rehearsal, and Miss Reynolds, our coach, had him and Carrie do a scene over. It was one where I prefer not to remember any details. But what did stick in my mind was when Miss Reynolds said, "Try that again, Carrie and Steve. A little more *emotion* this time."

That was bad enough but when Steve's face actually lit up at that idea, I didn't think I could live through it. I looked at my watch, out the window, on the floor—anywhere but at the stage. I told Eloise about it.

"He looked happy, El. *Happy!*"

"Well, for gosh sakes, Mag, he's human."

"That just proves it."

"Proves what?"

"That he should only look happy if it's me he's looking at."

"Oh, boy." She blew out her breath. "If six guys were lined up, each one drooling to get a date with you, Mag—"

"Stop fantasizing," I interrupted.

"No, now listen. So those six drooling guys are ready to paw you. How would you feel?"

"I'd die."

"Yeah, but you'd probably die happy, Mag, and you're supposed to be in love with Stevie, so there."

I thought about that. "I'm not sure . . . unless Stevie was one of those six."

He never came close to it. We were practically only on Hi terms for the whole time. Once, though, Stevie was walking in the corridor with *Her*, and he gave me the most wonderful Hi I ever got in my life.

The thing was, though, the ones who had principal roles in the play were like a select group. I mean they'd have private rehearsals, and lots of times they'd take up a whole table at lunch, all talking real excited. That's when I could walk by and Stevie wouldn't notice. Eloise said I was too mousy for him to notice me.

"You gotta use pizzazz, Maggie."

"I don't have any," I told her.

"You do, too, and if you think you don't, you have to pretend."

I gave her a sidelong look. "You're doing so well yourself?"

"Sure I am," she answered with assurance.

If I didn't know better I'd think from the way she said it that she was Miss Oakdale of the Year. Eloise does have your All-American blue-eyed, blond-haired, upturned nose good looks. She also happens to have a terrific shape. However, she is taller than anyone in school except for a couple of ninth grade boys on the basketball team. By the end of the seventh grade, the only attention she got from the opposite sex was questions about her strategy and tactics in intricate sports plays. So I couldn't see that, if she was pretending, it did any good. Well, maybe what counted was how a person sees herself. But I sure didn't see myself as Miss Pizzazz of any year.

No matter. I considered my seventh grade year a success. After all, I had established contact with Stevie, and my marks were good, too. I even got straight A's in social studies.

So now I was in the eighth, and extracurricular sign-up day had been announced for Thursday after school, and I was going to write my name large and clear for the Dramatics Club. A new school year meant new opportunities. I was determined that this year Stevie Garber and I were going to get to know each other in a more meaningful relationship, which was going to be the absolute, ultimate end!

Wednesday, in my homeroom, I was getting ready to go to lunch when Miss Randall called me over to her desk.

"From your seventh grade record, Maggie, I see you did very well in social studies."

I don't know why, but I suddenly got a radar message she was going to tell me something ominous.

She gave me this big smile like I was supposed to get elevated to cloud nine with the compliment, and then she said, "I expect you'll continue the same way this year. That's why I would like you to help us in the tutor-aide program."

I had seen notices about it on the bulletin board outside the auditorium, the lunchroom, and the gym. That was a new plan where people who were doing well in a subject could help the handicapped kids in our school, if they needed it. That included every type of handicap that was ever discovered, like cerebral palsy, retarded, wheelchair people—the whole bit. But I tell you, even if I got straight A's in everything, I'd never volunteer for that. I mean, it's one thing to feel sorry for these kids but something else again to watch them at close range. No matter how anyone feels, it's gross.

We had this boy, Joey, in our class last year. I don't know the name of his disability, but he used those metal canes that were partially attached to his wrists like bracelets, and he slurred his speech besides. The kids couldn't look at him. It was like they were afraid his ailment would rub off on them. A couple of boys had no sensibility at all, and when poor Joey tried so hard to make the right sound and something different came out, I saw those kids poke each other and hold back laughing like it was a riot. I certainly don't see anything funny about it, but just because I feel that way doesn't mean I would want to be near him.

Miss Randall waited for me to say something after she laid that request on me, but I was holding my breath just thinking about what I might be in for.

"You know about the program, don't you, Maggie?"

I nodded.

"Could you plan to stay tomorrow after school for an orientation session?"

Tomorrow after school! That was Sign Up for Dramatics Club with Stevie Garber Day! No way in the world was I going to give up the chance that was waiting for me in the gym. No, no, I shouted in my head.

Miss Randall looked at me questioningly, waiting for my answer.

"Uhng, phmm." I swallowed and finally let out that breath. But on its way out I knew I was trapped.

If I refused she would think, that wouldn't be Marge Thayer's daughter.

My mother is Marge Thayer, secretary to the principal of Woodrow Wilson Junior High. And my conscience is the type that makes me feel if I make one wrong move, my mother could get fired.

And it's not that I blame my mother. Honest, at home she's angel cake and ice cream. But on the outside she is conscious of how it would look if I did anything that wasn't a thousand percent. The only thing that saves me from getting neurotic is that Milt Sparnock's father is the assistant principal. I don't even want to envision what it's like for Milt.

"Good, Maggie. I knew I could count on you."

What'd I say? Did I say I'd do it? My head must have bobbed when I let out my breath, which she must have interpreted as yes. If my mother had to have a career, why couldn't she have chosen something that wouldn't put her in my school!

"Room six-B right after the final bell," Miss Randall was saying.

I'm gonna die. I don't want to be a tutor to anyone, least of all some miserable-looking sick kid. I gave Miss Randall my grateful and happy smile, but believe me, it was strictly on the surface.

I got out of there with my head feeling numb. Eloise was waiting for me.

"You look awful, Mag," she said as we started walking down the corridor. "What happened?"

I couldn't speak. I was raging inside.

"Miss Randall say something?"

All I could do was nod.

"Well, what? Talk to me!"

"El"—I nearly burst into tears—"she wants me on the tutor-aide program. That disgusting program, and I'm supposed to show up tomorrow after school. After school, El! You know where I *should* be then!"

"Hey, Mag," she said softly and reached out for my arm. "Don't worry about the sign-up. I can fill in your name."

I was poking around in my purse for some Kleenex. "Yuh, but, El, that was going to be one of my opportunities to see Stevie!"

"You'll make the club, and you'll see him all year."

Sometimes Eloise can make you believe the sun will shine on the day you plan to go to the beach even if the weatherman promises a thunderstorm. But the disappointment over missing Stevie was more than even Eloise could lift me out of.

"How do I know? Maybe that stupid tutor thing will conflict all year."

"Aw, Mag, don't look at it that way." She pressed my arm. Then she waited a decent interval and asked me, "What kind of a handicap will you get?"

"El! That sounds as if it's catching."

"You know I didn't mean that."

"You might as well have, for the way it's going to turn out." I let out a deep sigh. "I don't know which one I'll get stuck with. What difference does it make? They're all bad."

Eloise made some kind of a sound that I knew was supposed to be comforting, but it didn't help.

We made it to the cafeteria and inched our way through the mob scene to the food line.

"Shall we take the beef stew?" Eloise asked.

"Yecch. That's made with horse meat. Let's try the pizza."

"That's just as bad. It's made with cardboard." She looked along the counter. "Spaghetti?"

"Okay, I feel reckless," I said, reaching for it.

I know I could get a better deal if I let my mother make sandwiches. But last year I thought the in-thing was to eat school food, and this year Mom decided it was a good way to show trust and loyalty to where she works by eating their food. Well, Milt Sparnock does—probably has to—so I guess I can survive it, too.

We found a table with a couple of our friends, Gail Sheppard and Debbie Reinhall.

"Have you guys heard the latest disaster?" Debbie makes disaster announcements regularly.

"We're eating it," Eloise informed her.

"Besides that," Debbie said.

"Sure," I moaned, "the very latest disaster just happened in my homeroom. Miss Randall appointed me a tutor aide."

"Oh, Maggie, that's awful," Gail said sympathetically.

"That's a minor disaster compared to the one I'm going to tell you about," Debbie said.

"Is it national or local?" Gail asked.

"Not only local, but something that will affect us right here at the W. W. Junior High School!"

"Like what?" I asked offhandedly, picking at the spaghetti. "What could be a worse tragedy than mine?"

"Like really bad news. Last night my mother informed me that certain programs were going to be dropped from the Oakdale School system."

I couldn't believe my luck! "You mean the program for the handicapped!"

"The way I heard, it was just extracurricular activities like art, music, drama, baseball—"

"Dramatics Club!" "Baseball!" Eloise and I sputtered simultaneously.

"Where did you hear that rumor, Debbie?" Eloise demanded.

"From Carol Grey's mother. Mr. Grey is running for the school committee, and he says the taxes in Oakdale are too high and the only way to lower them is to get rid of all the junk."

"Junk!" Eloise and I nearly choked on the word.

Without the sports program Eloise would need psychiatric help, and if the Dramatics Club went, my slim chances for even a make-believe-possible love scene with Stevie Garber would go right with it. And I'd be left with nothing but a depressingly handicapped situation.

Eloise slammed her fist on the table. "They wouldn't dare! Sports are—sports are—cripes, that would be undermining future physical fitness leaders of America!"

"You think you've got a problem." Debbie looked at Eloise as if she were part of the cardboard in her pizza. "My mother says if anything gets removed from our curriculum I will go live with my father in Florida where, she says, the schools have everything. I will absolutely perish if I have to leave here."

"Say listen, kids. I just thought of something." Eloise was straining to find a silver lining. "It's going to be up to the new school committee to make changes, and they won't take office until January. So at least we've got until then to have our programs, and maybe those people won't get elected anyway. *Somebody's* going to be on our side."

That was barely hopeful, but I had to accept crumbs.

Debbie looked relieved. "Say, then my mother won't have any excuse to send me to Florida." Then as an afterthought she frowned and said, "Not that living with my mother is a bargain."

I ate half my lunch, and Eloise and I left together for our next class.

"That whole thing Debbie told us was a rumor. A malicious rumor." Eloise sounded as if she was blaming Debbie for making the whole thing up.

"Yeah. Rumor," I echoed gloomily.

It was definitely worse for me than it was for the others. First I'm a tutor to some drooling individual and next I'm denied that meaningful relationship I've been looking forward to for a whole year. Problems like these I didn't need to complicate my life.

Chapter Two

"I'll race you home," Eloise challenged me as we were leaving the building.

"You mean we're not going to talk about what's really bothering us?"

"Correct."

"Maybe you're right."

"I think we should work off some of our misery in a physical way."

"You're kidding, of course."

"Why should I be kidding?"

"Like, for instance, the cleanup squad would be locating parts of me all over town from the splatter my body would make as I dropped from exhaustion."

"Exertion, you mean, That's your trouble. You need more exercise. I'll jog you home—no race."

"No."

"C'mon." She pulled my sleeve, and for the next three blocks Eloise did a lot of slowing down, I did a lot of hard breathing, and then we walked to the intersection where we go in different directions.

"Well, see you here in the morning."

"Yeah. Same time, same channel."

"Don't worry about a thing now."

"Who's worrying?"

"Atta-girl. Bye."

"Bye."

She was saying good-bye walking backwards, suddenly she ran toward me and we hugged each other. That's not our usual method of parting every day, but considering what we had found out, the hug gave us consolation. After another real hard one, we separated and looked at each other unhappily.

Then Eloise said, almost as if she was trying to convince herself, "Mag, it's not going to happen."

"Oh, El, I hope you're right."

"Call me later, Mag."

"Sure."

"Bye."

"Bye."

Mom was already home when I got in, which meant she got a ride with one of the other secretaries. If I get in ahead of her, I'm supposed to check up on Robby before I do anything else. Or, if Tommy, my other brother, gets in before I do, it's his job.

Robby is six, and he gets home from school at two-thirty. That means he's alone for at least an hour, and to my mother that represents child abuse. You can see I inherit my sense of guilt from her. She wrestled with her conscience about working outside the home, to quote her, for the whole year before Robby was in kindergarten. And then she suffered, feeling that she abandoned him to a sitter until she got home. So now Tommy and I are the sitters. Except I'm usually it. With no pay.

Tommy, unfortunately, you can't always

count on. At the age of eleven he is very preoccupied with his own business. He has a bike-repair shop with a crew of one. Denny, his friend and employee, runs errands. Tommy won't tell us what he pays him—he says that's an invasion of privacy—but I suspect it's around twenty-five cents a month. They work in our garage, since our car is parked in the driveway when it's not being used. But Tommy is so engrossed in his corporation that the house could be on fire with Robby in it and Tommy would be blowing up inner tubes and straightening out spokes, or whatever he does. His big beef is that he doesn't have a phone in there.

"I can pay for it out of my profits, Dad. How about it?"

My father doesn't crack a smile. He's dead serious with Tommy as if he's discussing a shipment of merchandise with one of his business associates. Daddy has the biggest stationery and office supply store in Oakdale—and the biggest town hangout next to Bailey's Ice Cream Parlor. Which isn't bad, since I see Stevie in there once in a while. Next summer Dad said he'd let me work part-time. I hope Stevie doesn't go to camp or someplace.

"From a practical standpoint," Dad told Tommy, "you might want to wait to invest in a phone until you've been established for a year. Then you'll take inventory, see what your income tax will be, and figure your profit and loss."

Tommy got this look in his eyes like he was on the way to a triple-A rating in Dun & Bradstreet. That's the company that rates businesses according to how much money they make and how fast they pay their bills, and AAA is like in the billions. Tommy accepted Dad's idea but he still feels deprived of a phone. I heard him tell Denny he was thinking about applying for a government loan for necessary equipment. I nearly cracked up, but I didn't let on to him.

Anyway, that gives you an idea where Tommy's mind is, which doesn't make him Mr. Dependable to take care of his little brother except maybe in an emergency. I always hoped he'd never be put to the test. Once he was . . . but I'll get to that later.

My mother and Robby were sitting at the kitchen table enjoying a late afternoon snack. Robby's was milk and chocolate chip cookies, which I personally had made over the weekend. Actually, it was a joint venture with Eloise. We made a double batch so she could take some home.

"How are the cookies, Rob?" I asked him.

" 'Lishus."

"You mean luscious or delicious?"

"Both," he said reaching for another.

"Join us, Maggie." Mom was having tea and nothing.

She just verges on plumpness, and I think she has tremendous willpower to resist my cookies.

"Don't mind if I do."

"Have a good day?"

"Terrible, Mom."

"Honey!" She sounded and looked as if she thought I'd been assaulted. "What happened?"

I poured myself a glass of milk, sat down with them, and reached for a cookie.

"Well, it wasn't so horrible itself; it was more the threat of what's coming?"

"What is coming? When?" She frowned and waited as if I were going to announce the date of an enemy invasion.

"Tomorrow. Tomorrow I am going to be oriented on the tutor-aide program for handicapped students, and after that I'm going to have to be a tutor to one of them, and I just lost my appetite." I put the cookie back on the plate.

Robby grabbed it.

Mom gently put her hand on Robby's and said, not looking away from me, "That's the last one, Robby. More will spoil your supper. Maggie, I'm ashamed of you."

"Oh, Mom," I whined. "Why did it have to be me?"

"Maggie, I am doubly ashamed. You sound as if *you* were handicapped."

I made a grouchy sound.

"It's a fine thing to do," she went on, "and it's an honor to be chosen."

I twitched my mouth. Why couldn't she tell me I had too many other responsibilities to take on anything else? Such as looking after Robby and assorted maid duties due to her working outside the home?

"Well, I just hope I don't get some weird case, that's all."

"You just be grateful you're healthy, and don't be so squeamish."

"It better not conflict with my extracurricular activities—and that's another thing!"

"What's that?"

"Mom, Debbie Reinhall said her mother told her that Carol Grey's mother told her that Mr. Grey—"

"Whoa. Whoa there. Just give me the facts, ma'am. Start again."

"The facts are that if we get a new school committee, they're going to cut our curriculum to the *bone* and there won't be *one decent* course left!"

"Honey, those aren't facts; they're rumors," she said. "I heard the same thing today by way of the office grapevine."

I felt an uncomfortable lump settling into my chest. "Mom, if you heard it, too, it's probably more fact than rumor. Do you think they'll really do it?"

"It's hard to tell. People are very upset about high taxes."

"What do you think they'll cut?" I must have been punishing myself to want an answer to that.

"Most likely the things that are the most costly, like—"

My eyes lit up. "The program for the handicapped? Those station wagons and vans they use must cost a bundle, Mom," I said hopefully.

She shook her head. "No, it would be only extracurricular subjects. Things like some sports programs and other after-school activities that teachers get extra pay for. For instance—"

"Never mind, Mom. I don't want to hear it."

"Honey, I'm not saying they will, but if it does happen, there's nothing we can do about it."

"You mean we just accept it?"

"*If* it happens, people will save money, and that's important, Maggie. You know that."

She got up from the table with her cup and saucer and took the cookie jar.

"Can't I have just one more?" Robby begged as if he were undernourished.

"Not one. You can go out and play, Robby."

"Can I have some later?"

"After supper."

"You make good cookies, Maggie," he said on his way out. "I hope nobody cuts you."

I almost laughed, but I wasn't quite in the mood. He's a nice little kid, I thought. I should remember that when I'm baby-sitting against my will.

My mother was rinsing out the dishes, and I wanted to talk to her some more about the handicapped thing. Not that I expected her to change her mind about how noble my tutoring would be, but I wanted to let her know how scared I felt.

"Mom."

"Yes, dear."

"I . . . ." I opened my mouth to say, Suppose I got a kid who didn't talk right or who looked funny, and yeech, I hated even to think about that, but Tommy's voice and the slamming of the front door announced his arrival.

"Mom! Mom, as an employer, don't I have the right to fire Denny?"

He charged into the room with a look so frantic that I wondered what crime Denny had committed.

"That depends, Tommy," she said.

My problem must have vanished from her mind.

"Mom, Denny is goofing off on company time!"

"Have you talked it over with him?"

"I sure have!" He sounded belligerent, and I could imagine how that "talk" went. "And you know what he said?" Tommy now sounded outraged. "That he was going to write to the State Labor Relations Board!"

"I don't know, sweetheart. Maybe you threatened him instead of talking things over. That's the best way . . . calmly and fairly." She looked at him questioningly.

He gave her a look that anyone with half an eye could see was guilt-filled. Which you certainly didn't often see on his face. He definitely doesn't take after me in that regard.

"Well . . ." His argument seemed to peter out. "He—he better get on the ball." He stuffed a cookie in his mouth, knowing he had lost that little debate with my mother.

I was deciding whether to discuss what was on my mind in front of Tommy when the phone rang. I grabbed it. It was my father.

"Hi, Maggie. How's my girl?"

My father doesn't make it a practice to get a midafternoon health report, so I figured there was some really important reason why he called.

"I'm fine, Daddy. Want to talk to Mom?"

"Right, sweetheart. I'll see you later."

I handed her the phone, which is on the kitchen wall. She had already dried her hands and the dishes, and picked it up.

"Yes, Hal . . . Yes . . . School committee, yes. . . . Oh, I'm sorry."

No! They did it already!

"They want you to take her place? Oh, my. Well, of course, dear. Why not? . . . Yes . . . yes . . . I'll see you at the usual time. Bye, dear." Mom hung up, and there was a sort of stunned but happy expression on her face. "Well . . . well, what do you know?" It was as if she was experiencing some kind of dreamy, unexpected pleasure.

"Everything okay, Mom?"

"I—I think so. I mean . . ." She was still looking out into space.

"Well, *what*?" I was getting nervous.

She faced me, smiling broadly—back to earth. "Fran Harrington, who was running for school committee, had to drop out because she's been transferred out of state. *And* the group that was backing her wants Daddy to run in her place!" She couldn't keep back the joy she was feeling. "Your father. How about that?"

"Dad, running for school committee!" Tommy slammed the refrigerator door and almost dropped the carton of milk that was in his other hand. "Wow. I'm gonna be his campaign manager. Oh, boy. When is he coming home?"

Mom gave a giddy kind of laugh. "He has to go to City Hall and fill in the necessary papers and get the signatures of certain people—a lot of formalities, and then he'll be home."

Tommy was still standing with the milk carton in his hand. "Dad in politics!"

"Oh." Like lightning struck, I thought of Carol Grey. Her father was for cutting all those activities, and my father was going to be running against him. Wonderful. Terrific. Fantastic. I grabbed the phone off the hook and punched the buttons, making the familiar tones of Eloise's telephone number.

"Eloise," I screamed into the mouthpiece. "A burning issue has just come up!"

"Like what?"

"El, about those cuts?"

"They couldn't move so *fast!*" She ended on a shriek.

"Well, yes. In the right direction. Get this, Eloise Barton. My father has been requested to run for school committee due to a sudden vacancy caused by the removal of Fran Harrington, one of the candidates."

My mother and Tommy were standing there rapt, like an appreciative audience. Tommy was still clutching the milk carton.

"Your father! We're in." Eloise's tone changed to squealing joy. "We can depend on *him* to do the right thing."

"You bet your life!"

"Maggie baby, you know what this means? It means you and I are going to raise money for his campaign. We'll organize block parties, we'll have ice cream–eating contests, we'll have Jog for Hal Thayer Day. *Nothing* will stand in the way of his election!"

I listened and loved her to death. "Okay, I'll pass that on, El."

"Keep me informed, Mag. I'll be waiting at the phone all night."

We hung up. Mom and Tommy hadn't moved, and the three of us grinned at each other. Dad was going to be a pretty important person in town.

"Hey, I gotta tell some of my pals." Tommy came back to the present like someone plowing through a fog.

"Are you planning to take the milk with you?" Mom asked him.

"Oh." He looked at the carton as if it had been placed there while he was sleepwalking. "Well, I'll just have a fast one." He poured a glassful, and I suddenly felt up to having a cookie.

Chapter Three

We were all still covered with this rainbow aura when my father came home. We heard him parking the car and almost knocked each other out trying to get to him first as he opened the door. And when he did, he looked like a kid who walks in the house on his birthday and tons of friends yell, "Surprise!" He had this special look for Mom, and he said like he didn't believe it, "Marge, I'm running for public office." Then they got into this big embrace. The whole deal really meant a lot to us.

After that there were a million questions. Robby thought if Daddy was going to "run," couldn't he run, too? After all he owned a perfectly good pair of jogging shoes.

Then Tommy wanted to make sure Dad would let him be his campaign manager. My father as usual didn't bat an eyelash.

"We'll need all the help we can get, Tom," he said.

"Eloise has already volunteered her services for fund-raising things," I told him.

He grinned. "Great. Now if I can get the rest of the Woodrow Wilson eighth grade in my corner, I'll have it made."

"What's fund-raising?" Robby wanted to know.

Daddy explained it was to raise money for publicity, and while he was trying to get across what "publicity" meant, Tommy's business mind was clicking with ideas.

"Oh, boy, Dad! How about bumper stickers? I can give them out to all my bicycle customers? And you know what? I'll turn all my job profits over to the campaign fund. And T-shirts, Dad, T-shirts. 'Hal's Your Pal.' Is that great? Is it?"

Daddy appreciated Tommy's generous offer to turn over his profits and told him so. "But I'm not sure that 'Hal's Your Pal' is quite the tone we want. We'll have to work on a slogan. But before that, Ken Berns—he was helping Fran Harrington—thinks we should get a brochure out right away. Which means we have to decide tonight what to include."

"You mean like what issues you're running on, Daddy?" I asked, getting warmed up to the subject.

"That's right." He sounded pleased.

I beamed at how I impressed him with my awareness.

"I have the same point of view that Fran has," Daddy went on. "That's why her people are behind me, of course, but the brochure has to reflect Hal Thayer, not Fran Harrington."

"Naturally," Mom said. "We'll make a list of the issues in order of importance."

"I'll get my notebook, Dad," Tommy was halfway out of the room when my mother stopped him.

"We'll work on it after we eat," she told him firmly.

Which was a good thing, the way it turned out. It gave me a little more time before I found out what Fran Harrington's point of view was and how identical it was with my father's.

We got settled in the family room after we hurriedly did the dishes. I kept thinking how great Eloise was going to feel when I told her that things were moving right along the way we wanted them.

Then I heard Daddy say, "There is no question but that taxes are the primary concern of Oakdale's residents, and as a school committee member, my obligation to my constituents would be to cut waste in the schools."

I felt a thud inside me. Like a magnet, my eyes focused on Mom. She sensed what was in my mind, returned the look, and gave me an understanding nod.

"Hal"—she turned to my father—"a lot of parents feel strongly about keeping certain programs that they worked hard to get in the first place."

Good going, Mom.

"I'm talking about waste, Marge. In this town I know there is also a strong desire to eliminate frills and put more emphasis on basics."

I know I got pale. What's his idea of frills? I was about to ask him, but I couldn't. I lost my power of speech. I looked at Mom again. Tell him, Mom, tell him, my look said. Only thing was, her attention was on Daddy who sounded like he was making an oration.

"I think we should investigate the possibility of a compromise. I certainly don't want to be rigid, but we all know that some so-called electives are plain and simple nonsense." He looked at me, and I think I jumped. "Maggie, last year at Woodrow Wilson, didn't they have something called Critical Observation?"

I swallowed some saliva that had been accumulating and rediscovered my voice. "Yes, Daddy."

"And wasn't that in reality," he continued as if he were the D.A. in a murder trial, "watching television programs and then having a rap session afterward?"

I nodded, feeling he was going to sentence me to twenty years in solitary because I attended the Woodrow Wilson school. I didn't take the course, I wanted to shout in my defense, but I only looked at the floor feeling ashamed.

"You see, Marge, the cost of those TV sets alone was an unnecessary expense."

"That's true, Hal. But that doesn't mean that all electives or after-school programs aren't worth keeping."

"I agree. That's what a school committee is for—constantly to appraise, to evaluate . . ."

I'd had enough. I suddenly remembered I had to do some homework for one of my "basic" courses, and I asked to be excused.

I called Eloise.

"Eloise Barton, Thayer Campaign Committee," she barked into the phone in answer to one ring.

"We've been framed," I groaned.

"I'm afraid to ask."

"I'm afraid to tell you."

"Tell me gradually."

"Well, you remember what Debbie said Mr. Grey wanted to do?"

"Not the *sports programs!*"

"Who knows?"

"Your own father!"

"Don't rub it in."

"The Dramatics Club, too?"

It's not that I'm superstitious, but I felt I'd rather not say.

"What do we have to look forward to?" She sounded as if our futures just got permanently blacked out.

"For you, jogging. For me, a disabled, handicapped, mentally retarded, emotionally sick tutee."

"What's a tutee?"

"The opposite of a tut*or.*"

Silence.

"See you in the morning, Mag."

"Yeah. Same time, same channel."

Chapter Four

"El," I said to her on the way to school the next day, "maybe we'll be lucky and he'll lose the election."

"If he loses, Mr. Grey gets in. Either way we're dead."

For the first time in our lives we walked halfway to school without saying a word. I was thinking that up to yesterday I was part of a fairly normal family. Well, not exactly normal, considering we have only one car, one telephone number, and I have to share a bathroom with two boys. Unless one of us is willing to walk down to the laundry room on subground level for our morning and evening ablutions. There's no tub or shower there, and the sink is beside the washing machine, so it's hardly worth the trip, and nobody does it.

Take Eloise. She has a john all to herself, and when company comes to her house they have this private little toilet and sink arrangement on the first floor, and she can leave her own bathroom upstairs a complete mess and nobody sees it or cares. That's what comes from having a father who's a lawyer instead of a poor stationery and school supply store owner like mine. Of course Gail has it even better. Her father is a doctor. Besides her private bathroom and a "children's telephone" number, she has a TV in her own room!

How could I have ever been thrilled about Daddy running? I bet when my mother thinks it over carefully, she'll see it's going to be a big hassle. That morning she was already torn between being glad for Daddy and unhappy about the way I felt. Besides that, she was talking about having a family portrait in the brochure, and the big question was, should it be on page one or at the end? Maybe I'd make a disgusting face when the photographer said, "Smile," and Dad would lose some votes. From all I hear, people's prejudices influence their voting, and plenty of them wouldn't want to vote for someone who had a daughter with a disgusting face.

A block away from school, Eloise broke the silence. "Maggie, we've got to pull ourselves out of this. Let's list the good things."

"Sure. In five years we'll be off to college and we will have forgotten all about our deprived adolescence."

"Depraved, you mean."

"Right. Depraved."

"Seriously, Mag, we do have four months before the new committee will come in and start to make changes."

I sighed, a real deep one. "That's my one salvation, El."

"Keep thinking of it, Mag. It'll get you through the day."

"I wish you hadn't said that."

"I thought it was a very positive thing to say."

"Not if you were me, you wouldn't. The end of *my* day I get oriented."

"Oh, I'm sorry about that, Maggie. But maybe it won't be as bad as you think."

I didn't make the obvious answer. Of course it would be as bad as we both thought, and knowing that made the anticipation worse. Also, I hadn't gotten over having to miss the Dramatics Club sign-up.

The only halfway decent thing that happened that Thursday was overhearing a conversation in the corridor on the way to my last-period class.

"You mean it, Steve? They have scholarships for that?"

The question came from behind me. The answer was from the dark, chocolaty voice that transforms me to mush.

"Well, sure," he said. "Theater Arts is a big deal in some places."

"Like jerkwater colleges, you mean."

"No, my Dad says Yale and even Harvard have special programs."

"Cheez. Maybe I should try out for the Dramatics Club . . . you never know."

I figured that wasn't Stevie's friend Cooper or he'd have tried out last year just to be near that Carrie person. Some dumb reason. At least Stevie was interested in acting for a good purpose. I mean he was looking ahead to his future. I reasoned out very logically that for me to try out to be near Stevie was in a completely different category than for Cooper to want to be near *that girl*.

After the last bell sounded, Eloise and I started the trek down to six-B, and we looked at each other wordlessly.

"I have to stop for a second," I said as we got to the girls' room. It was more for psychological than any other need.

"Notice everything at the sign-up, El," I instructed her when I came out. "Who he talks to—female, that is. And who else signs up—female, that is."

"I will, Mag. I'll watch him like a hawk."

She held onto my arm as we walked downstairs as if I was on my way to the operating room. What I really needed was a brain transplant. Swap mine for one that would keep me from getting into situations I didn't like.

The door was open, and we heard voices from inside. Eloise patted my shoulderblade. "Right after sign-up I'll come back and wait for you right here."

I didn't move.

"Go ahead, Maggie. It can't last forever."

I slowly took a couple of steps and then turned to give her one last look. A sad one.

Room six-B is next to the furnace area and probably used to be a utility closet, judging from its size. Actually it's where slow learners go when they need extra help, but they never have more than three kids in there at a time, so it has all the space it needs. There's a table, some bookshelves lining two of the walls, some chairs, and no windows. Sort of dungeonlike. and I had visions of spending gruesome hours down there with whoever I was assigned to.

Miss Randall was sitting at the table. Mrs. Hall, the guidance counselor, and Mr. Kahn, my math teacher, were beside her. I hadn't had any contact with Mrs. Hall since she's the ninth grade guidance counselor who you discuss your high school program with. Before then, if you know her it's because you've been in some kind of trouble. Up to today, I hadn't been.

Mr. Kahn is real cool. Math is not my favorite subject, but on account of Mr. Kahn I look forward to it. Physically he's not your Robert Redford type—or your Stevie Garber type, for that matter. He's not even good-looking. Tall, but skeleton skinny. His face has the kind of bone structure that looks like those angles in abstract art. And he wears glasses with thick lenses. But he's nice. And he has a sense of humor. Like the first day of school he gave us calculators, and a couple of boys thought that was the password for a soft A.

"This is a great little gadget, guys," Mr. Kahn told them, "but you have to push the right buttons. And the calculator doesn't tell you which ones they are. Get it?"

What I'm trying to say is, he teaches you stuff, you have a lot of respect for him, but he's easy to laugh with.

I looked around and noticed four other recruits already there. Two girls and two boys. I knew the boys, Harvey Ferris and Milt Sparnock, who was in the same boat as me—forced labor.

Miss Randall gave me her smile again and said, "Maggie, would you close the door, please? Since we're all here now, we can get started."

As I went back to the doorway I got a glimpse of Eloise. She was still there, huddled against the wall like she was part of the plaster. She saw me, raised her hand and wiggled her fingers in a sort of wave. It didn't seem to boost my spirits. I only looked at her, not really focusing, and then closed the door.

Mrs. Hall opened up the séance and asked us if we all knew each other. Some of us didn't. She introduced us all around and thanked us for coming. As if we had a choice.

Then she went into her spiel. "As you know, this year we have seventeen boys and girls at Woodrow Wilson who have come from special schools. They are handicapped in many different ways. Some are visually impaired, two have hearing deficiencies, some are in wheelchairs, one is mildly retarded, and two have minor seizures."

Seizures! Not in front of me, they better not! Also, to be visually impaired and to have a hearing deficiency, I've always known as blind and deaf, but if she wanted to be fancy, okay.

She continued. "I've been very pleased with the way these students have adapted to us. In some cases, however, not all of *our* students have adapted as well to them. Mrs. Williams, our principal, Mr. Kahn, Miss Randall, and I have come up with a plan we hope will improve matters. Perhaps where attitudes haven't been as positive as they might be, it is because those boys and girls haven't had any exposure to others with handicaps. We know it takes time and understanding." She stopped and looked us all over. We nodded like robots. Then it was Miss Randall's turn.

"We thought a small number of you could start the ball rolling by treating the newcomers with special consideration. They need that at least as much as they need additional help in academic subjects. A good way to start is to have sensitive people like yourselves help in many ways. For example, in the lunchroom as well as tutoring. In other words, we think you will feel a special responsibility that will be beneficial to them as well as to you and the rest of the school." Then she asked, "Any questions at this point?"

"When will we do the tutoring?" Harvey Ferris asked Mr. Kahn.

"During your free period, which we will work out with each of you individually," he said.

That was a break. I wouldn't have to stay after school and miss my club. But who needs to give up a free period?

Miss Randall was talking again. "Now remember, people, this is on a trial basis. If you find you aren't comfortable with your assigned partner, feel free to discuss any problem you have. We invited you five in particular, and we hope we'll get more volunteers, because we feel you are most likely to succeed. We know you by reputation and scholastic record. . . . Mr. Kahn do you want to start?"

Mr. Kahn landed his gaze on Harvey. "Harve, my little genius, you get first crack at clarifying fractions into decimals for John Rossman. He is in a wheelchair, he speaks clearly without mumbling, not like some of us others, and he's apt to give you a run for your money. In fact, if you play your cards right, he might explain to you the intricate workings of his motorized contraption. You'll be astounded. Here is the assignment and schedule for your first meeting. Check it out and holler if there's a time conflict."

Harvey came up to the table and took the papers as Mr. Kahn called one of the girls and ran through some instructions for her. Miss Randall called the other girl and Milt and told them what they had to do while I shivered inwardly, realizing she must be saving the most barbaric for the last.

"Maggie?" Miss Randall invited me to the table, and I felt my skin flaming. "We have an especially nice seventh grade girl for you. Doreen Marshall. She is blind, and the particular reason she needs you is that her social studies textbooks haven't come through yet, either in Braille or on recordings."

Blind. That's what she said. Not even visually impaired. If there was an opening in the floor big enough for me to drop into and disappear, I'd have used it.

"Does that sound like something you'd care to do?" Miss Randall was actually asking me that.

She had to be kidding. Anyone could see I'd been panting to do this all my life.

"Well, I could try." I said it bravely but without a shred of courage to back it up.

"It may sound like a big order, but I believe you can fill it."

I thought of my mother. It's an honor, she had said. I'm not worthy, Mom, I told her in my mind. I quit right now.

But I can't do that. She'll get fired. . . . Oh, they won't fire her for that. Why didn't I come right out with it, then? I'm not interested, Miss Randall. Thanks just the same.

I pushed the glassy look out of my eyes. "I'm sure I can, Miss Randall," I lied.

"I'm glad, and you will be too, Maggie. You could start tomorrow in B Block, your free period. I'll tell her to wait for you in room two-twelve. She'll be ready for Chapter Three in *This Is America's Story*. Here's a copy you may use."

Everyone was leaving. "Good-bye, Miss Randall."

"Good-bye, Maggie."

Not one of those math, English, and social studies brains said one word or even looked in a way to give the impression they weren't a hundred percent in favor of doing this stuff. I don't believe it. They all have to feel like I do. It's not humanly possible to feel any other way. They're acting, that's what. They should all go out for the Dramatics Club. The four-month Dramatics Club, before it gets whammied.

"Good-bye, Harvey, Milt, Jennifer, Anne . . . Miss Randall."

Eloise was out in the hall. She jumped toward me. "How was it?" she said anxiously.

"Was Stevie there?"

"Yes. What did you get?"

"You won't believe. Did he say anything to you? Like, ask for me?"

"No. What did you get?"

I didn't expect him to ask for me. I swallowed, I deep-breathed, I gasped, and finally I said it: "A blind girl."

"Blind! You mean she can't *see?*"

"That's the usual situation."

"Oh, Mag, the poor thing!"

I gave her a funny look and felt ashamed. I hadn't given a thought to anything except my own discomfort. Well, if anything, that was going to make it worse. How was I going to be able to read to her when I had to overcome not only my squeamishness but now my sympathy?

We started up the stairs and clutched each other's arm as if we needed support to stand up. We got outside and looked at each other with the same tortured expression. The sign-up, Stevie, girls breathing down his neck—my mind had no room for that.

Without a word passing between Eloise and me, we started walking with our eyes closed, opening them only at the street intersections for the rest of the way home. It was scary.

Chapter Five

"Mom. Are you home? Wait'll you hear! She's blind!" I ran into the kitchen where my mother was just reaching for the wall phone. She dropped the receiver as if it had burned her fingers, letting it swing on its cord.

"Who—is blind?" Her face was pale, and she seemed frightened to let the words out, not really wanting to hear the answer.

"Doreen Marshall." I said the name as if it was somebody we'd known for years and wasn't it terrible what just happened to her.

"Who?" Lines showed across her forehead, but her voice sounded a little relieved. She looked as if she was trying to place Doreen.

"The handicapped girl I have to tutor."

She let out her breath. "Maggie, you terrified me there for a second." She put the receiver back on the hook.

"I didn't mean to, Mom. But,"—I shuddered—"blind."

"Honey, don't think of it as something upleasant that you *have* to do; it's a wonderful thing to be *able* to do." She reached for the phone again. "Have a snack, dear. I have to call some people who are going to help Daddy in his campaign."

"Mom, we have to talk about that." My voice was full of the anxiety I felt. "Are we going to let Daddy ruin our school?"

"Sweetie, what a thing to say. Whatever he does will be for the benefit of the community, and it's going to work out all right—you'll see."

My own mother! Dr. Jekyll and Mrs. Hyde!

"Oh, hello, Trish." She got her connection. "What do you think about Laura Kaplan for publicity? . . . Great. I'll call her. And, Trish, remember when Hal got the stop sign put up at the intersection near the Vine Street Elementary School? Well, he's so modest he doesn't think that's worthy of mention, but I think things like that show his civic-mindedness and ability to take action."

Mom was creating the brochure as she spoke.

"I'm glad you agree, Trish. Yes . . . we'll meet here tonight . . . eight."

She turned her head away from the mouthpiece. "Maggie, honey, get me that pencil and pad from the counter, please."

I handed it to her. Eight committee people here tonight plotting a scheme to eliminate my now and future contact with the boy I'm in *love* with! Or maybe it was one person at eight o'clock who was going to do that. It didn't matter.

I made a peanut butter and jelly sandwich and put it on a tray with a glass of milk and two of the last four chocolate chips.

"I'm going to do my homework," I said as I left the room.

Honest, she was talking on the phone as if when my father won the election we'd be moving to Sixteen Hundred Pennsylvania Avenue, Washington, D.C. Yesterday she felt the same as I did about school programs being cut, and today she had a sparkle in her eyes as if America was facing its finest moment. I was so emotionally upset over the way things were going that I could call Eloise only once that night.

When I woke up the next morning I wasn't exactly ready to jump out of bed and happily greet the new day, either. I knew what was waiting for me during my free period in B Block.

I kept swallowing in quick succession to test for a sore throat. But, my luck, it felt fine. I thought I might fake a stomachache but I was hungry and didn't want to miss breakfast. So it looked like B Block had me in a squeeze play, as Eloise would say in baseball talk.

I met her on the corner.

"I have a theory, Mag," she announced. "People who have the grossest time in their early life have it made in their old age."

I gave her a tired glance, which she didn't happen to be looking at, and I said, deadpan, "That's beautiful, Eloise."

"No, I mean it. Look how bad things are for you now, Mag. That means you have great things to look forward to."

"You're a true pal, Eloise. For years I've been worried that I was going to have a tragic old age, and now you have given me hope."

"Well, I tried."

How I got through my classes until ten-thirty when B Block started I don't know, but it certainly wasn't due to any great willpower on my part. I mean, I was pure Jell-O through math, and social studies turned me into tapioca. When the bell rang I must have jumped twenty feet as if I'd never heard a bell ring before. I left the room and aimed myself in the direction of room two-twelve.

It took longer than it usually does to walk fifty yards, but I was in no hurry. I finally made it. The door was open, and I forced myself to look.

I thought the girl sitting at the desk was somebody else. I mean she looked regular. Normal. So I figured I must have stopped at the wrong room, and I checked the number on the door again. Two-twelve . . . right.

Then I stood back from the doorway, just looking. Her hair was in a short, layered cut, the color that oak leaves get to be in the fall. But it had a shine as if it was just shampooed, or like the sun was streaming on it. She had this healthy look—pink cheeks and pretty—real pretty. I had supposed she'd be wearing dark glasses, but she wasn't, and then I wondered which would be more distracting to me—the glasses or her bare eyes. Either I wouldn't be able to keep mine off hers, or I'd be scared to look at her at all.

She was sitting straight up and looking into space. Space was all she could see, of course. I wondered what space looked like to her. Was it gray, black, crowded, empty? But she couldn't tell gray from black. I remembered how Eloise and I walked home yesterday. I closed my eyes to recall the effect and to feel how it was for Doreen. Nothing. Nothing, no color, no objects, nothing. I hugged my books closer to my chest as if I was protecting myself from a rush of cold wind.

I didn't want to make any sound for fear it

would startle her. Besides I still wanted to stall starting the whole thing. I wondered, should I speak loud? There was nothing wrong with her hearing, though. Didn't I read somewhere that blind people have extra good hearing sense? Maybe I should whisper, then.

I took a step, which made the floor creak, and she turned her head toward the door.

"Maggie?"

I cleared my throat and said, "Yes." It came out as if I hadn't cleared my throat in the first place.

She said, "O—oh," in three syllables. It was more like a trill than a speaking sound. Then she put the fingers of her right hand to her left wrist. What she was doing, I learned later, was feeling the raised symbols on her Braille watch. She turned at a better angle toward where I was standing, and she smiled. It showed nice teeth.

"I know it's only a minute past when the period starts, but I was so excited about your coming, it seemed like hours waiting."

She said it not so much as if she was glad I'd come to read to her, but like she was glad I was there. It gave me a nice sensation, which surprised me. I walked to the desk and sat on a chair opposite her.

That brought me real close, and I got the craziest feeling I wanted to look around to see if anyone was watching—like I had nerve staring at her because she didn't know it.

"Have you read any of this stuff before?" I asked her, fumbling with the pages of the history book.

I realized I'd said "read" and then could have killed myself. She couldn't read it, and that was why I was there. What was the matter with me? While that was bouncing around in my brain, I was aware of her eyes. Her whole head was turned right at me, and you'd swear she could see. I mean, her eyes were open like she knew what she was looking at, and they were this real dark shade of blue. I kept gaping, and she said, "I've read the first two chapters. My mother and I went over them together."

She said the same word I did—"read"—and it didn't seem to bother her at all. I got off lucky that time.

I found Chapter Three on page forty-four. The title was "The French, Dutch, and English Explore North America and Establish Colonies."

"You had this last year, Miss Randall told me. I hope you won't be bored reading it again."

Bored wasn't exactly the way I would have described my feelings. "Oh, no," I said. "I like social studies."

"I'm glad, and I think it's very nice of you to—to do this for me." She smiled again.

I blushed and realized I had to answer everything she said out loud since she'd never know from any expression on my face what I had in my mind. "Oh, that's all right," I said, and then blushed again because I thought it was a pretty meaningless thing to say.

"The new chapter is about colonies in North America," she said. "I think it's on page forty-four."

I got an eerie feeling as if my head moved away from my neck and shoulders and then came back into place. She had some fantastic memory. I took a good breath and started to read. It was all about after Spain, Portugal, and those other countries started their own explorations.

Then later the book said, "As the map on page forty-two shows," and I didn't stop reading until it was too late. As the map on page forty-two *shows!* How could I have said that out loud? That had to be making Doreen feel horrible. I'm going to tell Miss Randall to forget it. This definitely is not for me.

"I guess I'd better be typing out some notes for homework," Doreen said right at that point. She bent over to the floor beside her and got very busy lifting something. I thought what I just read must have disturbed her and she was hiding her face from me. Then she straightened up and put something on the desk that looked like a small typewriter. From a folder she pulled out a piece of stiff paper and put it in the machine.

Her face didn't show a single trace that she was upset. That girl either had to be pretty tough on the inside or pretty clever at self-control.

Watching her, I hadn't gone on with the reading, and she must have wondered why. So then she said, "Oh, you've probably never seen a Brailler before. That's what this is called. It types out Braille symbols, see?"

She pressed down some keys that didn't have any letters on them the way ordinary typewriters do. These just had grooves where you'd put your fingers.

"See? Feel," she said, reaching out for my hand and moving my fingers along the top of her paper. It gave me chills. Not from the tiny raised dots, but on account of her self. She was so relaxed—as if there was nothing wrong, nothing missing. Not that she could pretend she wasn't blind, but she wasn't acting sorry for herself. Which, to me, was a big switch. Usually, don't people who can see feel very sorry for the blind?

"Every group of dots stands for a letter. All I have to do is feel it and I know what it says," she explained.

"What did you just type?" I asked her in awe.

" 'Check relief map for page forty-two—French explorations in America.' "

How could she do that so fast? How could she do practically anything? I was sure she could hear the throbbing noise in my heart. I was supposed to be helping *her*, and she was coming up with things I never heard of.

"Relief map?"

"That's what it's called. They're maps that are molded from heavy paper in the exact shape like the picture maps. Only it's not flat on the page like yours. It's raised so you can feel, like for instance, where mountains are. And then whatever we're supposed to know about it is in a separate Braille notebook. And that notebook is one of the things that hasn't come through for me yet."

"Gee." That was all I could say.

"I'll show it to you. It's in the resource room.

You know, the room upstairs that has some special material for blind kids."

It just rolled off her tongue the same way I might tell someone what you had to do to run for election. Like I could say, "publicity brochures," and she could say, "relief maps for blind kids."

"I'd love to see it," I said. "But I guess we have to finish this reading first."

"Sure. What time do you have lunch? Maybe we could go up there after, if we have the same lunch period." She looked at me again aiming her face at exactly the right direction. For a second I honestly thought the whole thing was some kind of a joke on me—that she wasn't really blind.

"Twelve-ten." I said it automatically but a hundred different questions ran through my head. How would she get to the lunchroom? How did she get around at all? Would I have to push her in a wheelchair or lead her by the arm? Miss Randall hadn't given me any clues. Instead, she had said, "You will find this a revealing experience." Plenty was getting revealed to me all right. I'd have to agree with her there. I was also getting hot and cold in rhythm like lights blinking on and off all over me.

"Oh, great. That's my lunch period today, too. Do you want to meet me by the wide entrance door? We can eat together and then go."

How did she know the entrance to the lunchroom had a wide door? And another thing, you know how it shows in your eyes the different ways you feel? How you can tell just by a person's eyes if they're angry or happy? Well, nothing different showed in Doreen's, but it didn't need to for me to notice that she was really keyed up about taking me to the resource room.

"Yuh, fine. By the wide entrance door," I repeated. I went on reading the chapter, and in a little while she felt her watch again.

"I've got English with Mr. Lee. I guess we'd better quit right now; he doesn't like anyone coming in even one second late. Do you have him?"

She leaned toward the floor, and when she got up I saw she had a cane in her hand. One of those long white ones with a red border at the bottom and a curved top. So that was how she got around. She picked up her typewriter by the handle and slid her notebook under that arm and with the other one aimed the cane on the ground in front of her.

"No, I have Mrs. Carstairs." I wondered how I could keep my mind straight to answer her question while I was dazzled by what I was seeing and discovering. It was so different.

I pushed my chair away from the desk and stood up. "Well, I've got French now. I'll see you later." I hoped she wouldn't be bothered by my using the word "see" so much. It just came out of my mouth like a natural thing.

"Right. See you." It came out of her mouth naturally, too.

I had to get ahold of Eloise and prepare her. How was that going to go over with her? We'd be eating with Gail and Debbie, too. How would it go over with them?

Eloise had math the next period, three rooms farther down from French. I spotted her ahead of me. "El," I shouted. "Wait up."

She turned and stopped. "How was it, Mag?" Her eyes pierced mine.

"Strange. Very strange. But listen, she's having lunch with us today."

"How come?" She looked as uneasy as I felt.

"She invited herself, I guess."

"Pushy, huh?"

"No . . . but no mouse."

She raised her eyebrows. "How do you think it'll go?"

"I just hope I don't have to feed her, that's all." The bell clanged over our heads.

"See you later, El," I said and ran back to French.

I thought of Doreen a couple of times during the period, but Madame Beauvais is no breeze, so I can't let my mind wander in her class. Matter of fact, I got so involved with the double negatives that when the bell rang and I looked at the clock, nothing special registered. Then I remembered and everything I touched fell out of my hands at least twice.

Chapter Six

If I had to give that lunchroom session a rating, I'd say F-minus. Not the way Doreen behaved. Her I'd give an A. But me. I'm the one who flunked.

I had waited for Eloise outside French.

"Maggie, are you sure you want to go through with this?"

"I'm sure I don't, but do I have a choice?"

We all but crept down the corridor, neither one of us being ready for the ordeal.

"Where is she going to be?"

"Outside the lunchroom. And listen, afterwards she wants me to go with her to something called a resource room. It's on the second floor, where they have special maps and things for the blind. I've never heard of the place. Have you?"

"Never."

"Will you come?"

"Today, you mean?"

"Today."

"I can't, Mag."

"You can't! What earthshaking event came up that you can't help out your best friend in a life-threatening situation?"

"I was going to tell you . . . Danny Cavelletti just asked me to shoot some baskets with him in the gym at twenty to one."

She looked miserable, and I couldn't be angry with her. Danny Cavelletti is the captain of the basketball team. He's one of the boys who's taller than Eloise, and she likes him, too. An opportunity like that didn't happen every day. I mean it wasn't like she was going to kill time, or with just anybody.

"Sure, El, I understand."

"You won't be sore?"

"Nah. I'll probably die, is what."

"Was it that bad being alone with her?"

"Well, no . . . it was just . . . funny. I'm not used to it yet."

"Should I not go with Danny? What do you think?"

"I think you should go. You'll beat the pants off him."

"Not the *pants*, Mag!"

We roared. Then we both felt better.

In between the mob of kids I looked down the hall to the cafeteria and saw Doreen. She was right by the wide entrance, her cane in front of her, clutching it with both hands and her head held as if she were searching the corridor and would know the exact second when I'd stand there even without my uttering a sound.

"There she is, El. Hi, Doreen," I called as we got closer.

Doreen's face lit up even if her eyes didn't, and her "Hi, Maggie" had a lit-up sound, too.

Eloise grabbed my arm. "She recognized your voice! Wow."

"Ssh," I whispered. Then I said, louder than I expected it to come out, as if it was to cover up the whisper, "This is my friend Eloise, Doreen."

Eloise acknowledged the introduction with a smile. I nudged her.

"Huh? . . . Oh. Hi, Doreen."

"Hi, Eloise." Doreen had waited for where the sound came from, and then she turned in the right direction before she spoke.

Eloise and I just stood there getting jostled by the incoming gang, waiting for Doreen to take the lead. I realized that was probably the best way to handle it, since she had more experience with people who can see than we ever had with people who didn't.

"Let's go," she said. Like I figured, she had no trouble at all getting to the right place.

"Smells like franks and beans," she said as if she liked it.

"That's one of my favorites," I told her. Actually it was one of the two or three things a year the nutrition department put out that was good. "My mother hardly ever makes it. She says that's next door to junk food, and she thinks we eat enough of that on the outside."

"I'm lucky. My mom isn't particular. She lets us have it Saturdays for lunch usually."

I hadn't thought about her family. I wondered who "us" meant. I also wondered how she was going to know when she got to the trays. And how would she know what else there was besides franks and beans? Would she have to smell everything first?

The line was pushing, and Doreen moved right along and reached over for a tray without even hesitating. She stopped in front of the frank-and-bean place, and Gertrude, our lunch lady, said, "You'll probably want a big spoon for those beans, honey. Mind they don't get on your pretty yellow blouse, now."

I cringed. Doreen would get upset over that, and mentioning the color of her blouse, which she couldn't see, too.

But Doreen grinned, and I swear she winked, saying to Gertrude, "Oh, I'm real neat."

I turned around to share my amazement with Eloise, who was standing there like a statue, gaping at Doreen. Then she came to, and we both shook our heads in wonder.

We chose what we wanted and looked around for an empty table. Gail and Debbie were waving and calling to us. I yelled, "Save three seats. Three!" I held up three fingers in case they couldn't hear me over the room noise.

"We're going to a table about eight paces straight and one to the right, Doreen," Eloise directed.

I gave her a special look. She would have been a big help in the resource room.

Doreen was still in front of us, and she walked to exactly where Eloise said, and we sat down. Gail and Debbie stared, not saying a word.

"Meet Doreen Marshall, girls. Doreen, that's Gail Sheppard and that's Debbie Reinhall. They're friends of ours.".

Afterwards I thought, Doreen couldn't know which was which just by my saying, "That's Gail and that's Debbie" but I was annoyed by their staring. This was getting to be a pain. It was enough I had my own queasy feelings to overcome, let alone having to feel responsible for anyone else's.

After I stared back at them, they said hi and we got busy eating. I'll admit it wasn't easy keeping our eyes off Doreen while she was involved in that feat. I mean, how *was* she going to keep food from falling all over her blouse? We all sneaked looks at her and then at each other, our hearts in our mouths. I knew she'd had plenty of practice at it, but just the same our plates weren't sectioned, and yet, she managed to locate what she wanted without too much trouble and aimed almost every bean into her mouth with no radical accidents. In fact, she even scooped all the juice from the sliced-peaches dish onto her spoon, and only a couple of drops spilled. That's finesse, I thought. Miss Randall couldn't have meant Doreen when she said we could help the handicapped kids in the lunchroom.

It was at that instant that Fate made Stevie Garber walk by our table. That was when my performance went from a passing grade to F minus. If I'd seen him coming I could have prepared myself. If I hadn't been taken by surprise I could've at least *appeared* casual even though I wouldn't have been feeling it. But this was unexpected. Our eyes met at the exact same second, and he sort of grimaced a smile and I turned purple. And promptly got a coughing fit.

Eloise started hitting me on the back. Gail and Debbie were saying frantically, "Are you okay, Maggie?" and Doreen jumped up from the table saying, "I'll get you some water."

"No, no," I choked out. I had visions of her getting stampeded by the entire student body as they were leaving the cafeteria at the end of lunch period. But with her finesse and my klutziness, she probably could have handled it better than I handled looking at Stevie.

He stopped, sort of hesitating, like he didn't know if he should call the emergency squad, when two boys, ninth grade dropout types, slapped Stevie on the back, and one of them said, "Hey, Garber, what did you do to the poor girl?"

The other creep added, "You do have power over women, Garber."

"Okay, knock it off, you guys." Stevie was embarrassed, I could tell, and I finally worked up my voice to say, "I'm okay."

I was wiping my eyes and straightening myself out, vaguely aware that he said something like "Take care." The two other boys gave him a nasty laugh, which he ignored as he walked away.

"For a minute, Maggie, I thought I was going to have to use the Heimlich maneuver," Gail said. "My Dad taught me how to do it if someone choked on food."

"A person can choke like that on only one drop of loose saliva," Eloise said quickly to cover for me. She knows my personal feelings for Stevie are just between her and me.

"Well, I'm glad you're all right," Doreen said, feeling her watch. "I think it's time we should go."

"Sure." I stood up, relieved to get out of there but wishing Eloise could join us.

"Oh, wow, it's twenty to one." Eloise bounced away from the table. "See you later, guys. Nice to meet you, Doreen."

"Same here." She smiled back at Eloise.

Gail and Debbie gave Doreen a friendly "so long," and we all left.

"I didn't think I was going to like it here," Doreen said as we headed for the stairway. "I mean, I wasn't used to going to school where everyone has sight, so I was kind of nervous about it. But you and your friends are so nice."

I was nice? I hoped it would never come out that I didn't do any volunteering for this job and that this morning I had wanted to quit.

"Where did you used to go to school?"

"A private boarding school just for blind children, but I didn't like being away from home. I missed my family. So we were all glad when this program began at Woodrow Wilson."

"You have brothers and sisters?" I asked.

"One brother, Jeff. He's my twin."

Her twin. Then, did that mean he was blind, too? Well, that was one question I sure wasn't going to ask.

"He goes to Holbrook, in our district. But there's no program for handicapped kids there. So I couldn't go."

Then he wasn't blind.

"But this is a great school."

Great school. How come she didn't know about the reason we had this tutor-aide program going? It had to be because she couldn't see when some of the kids were gawking, and if they laughed she didn't know they could be laughing at her.

Except for bumping into one door, Doreen could have got along without her cane to the second floor. She knew the way so well that she was leading me, since I'd never been there. The things that go on in your own school that you're unaware of.

The room was about twice the size of six-B, where I was the day before, with big windows and lots of sunshine. I thought how strange it was that the extra-help room for kids who could see was dark and gloomy and this one was inviting and pretty. I wondered if Doreen knew.

The resource teacher—who, Doreen told me, came in three times a week—was there, and Doreen said she wanted to show her friend the relief map. I got an awkward feeling when she referred to me as her friend. I didn't feel I had done anything to live up to it.

"Help yourself, Doreen. You know where they are. Just be sure you put them all back when you're through."

I thought that was fantastic, the way that teacher talked to her the same as the rest of us get talked to. I mean, she didn't have this special voice like you use when you're sorry for someone. I tried to watch both of them at the same time to see if Miss Sheehan, the teacher, was worried that Doreen would fall or mess things up, and I watched Doreen to see exactly what she was going to do.

She walked over and got the stuff as easily as . . . well, anybody. The maps were like she said; by feeling the raised parts, after she read the Braille key describing it in the book, she knew all the place locations. She said to me, "Ask me where someplace in South America is. Go on, ask me."

"Okay. Where is Colombia?"

I watched while she took her map, and her fingers started up at the top left side where I happened to remember Colombia really is.

"Here!" Her index finger pressed down on the right spot, and she was grinning a mile wide, so pleased with herself.

"Hey, Doreen, that's terrific."

"Now you do it," she said, handing me the map.

"How can I? I have to see the names."

Doreen broke up. Honest, she practically doubled up laughing.

"Well, of course, you're at a disadvantage," she said, calming down. "But I can show you how to do it."

How about that? *I* was at a disadvantage.

"Girls, if you have a class this period, you'd better start for it. You have about three minutes before the bell."

"Oh, gee," Doreen sounded disappointed.

"You can bring your friend another time. Now return the maps, Doreen, and scoot—both of you."

When we got down to the next flight Doreen asked. "Will you be reading to me again soon?"

"Of course," I told her. One by one I seemed to be losing the worries and reservations I'd had about her before.

"When is your free period on Monday?"

"It's in the afternoon, but Miss Randall said she'd work it out from both our programs," I said.

"Great. See you next week."

"See you," I repeated.

I watched her go down the corridor until she turned the corner. The thing I couldn't get out of my mind most was how come a girl with a handicap like hers could be so unbothered by it. I remembered last summer when I stepped on a piece of glass and I was scared to death I'd get blood poisoning, that gangrene was going to set in and they'd amputate up to my thigh.

Chapter Seven

That afternoon in social studies, Mr. Clayton started the session by reading from the *Weekly Tribune* the issues the school committee was concerned with. Then he got a discussion going during which people took sides for and against lowering the taxes and what would happen if.

I don't know where it came from, but I had a show of strength. I told him I chose to remain neutral since it was only fair for me to disqualify myself, considering my father was a candidate. He grudgingly accepted that, but I think the entire episode revealed the most utterly gross side of Mr. Clayton. I don't care if he gives me an A-plus for the year, I would still say that. I mean, like in half an hour it was all over school that Maggie Thayer's father was running for school committee. I was understandably very touchy about that subject.

"Maggie, I didn't know your father was a politician."

I must have heard that twelve times after class.

"Hey, Maggie, what side of the fence is your father on?"

That I heard at least twenty times before the end of the day.

"How heavy is your dad into the everything-must-go theory?"

I heard that only once. It was from Stevie, and we were both standing in front of the bulletin board where an announcement had been posted that tryouts for the first play would be in the auditorium Tuesday after school.

He kind of took me by surprise. I mean, I didn't know he was standing there. I wished there were some way I could be prepared or forewarned or something. I ought to start keeping a notebook of possible answers to any possible statements he might make at unexpected moments. At least he didn't make any reference to our last encounter in the lunchroom.

"Very." I answered his question. Which was honest if not clever.

"You serious?"

"Very," I repeated. I'd have to remember to strike that word from the notebook I was going to get that very day.

He paused, frowned, and then said like he couldn't believe it, "That must be tough for you that he wants to cut a program his daughter is interested in."

I wouldn't guarantee the color my cheeks got then. It wasn't the program his daughter was interested in; it was the person who was in the program.

"Oh, you know parents," I said, the words coming from nowhere. "No way can you control them . . . You get used to it."

He made a half-baked smile and wagged his head, which could have meant he thought my father was weird—or that I was. Some other kid started talking to him, and the best description of what I did is to say I faded into the background.

I was a wreck anticipating tryouts, and I couldn't decide what to wear. I'd been jinxed for the sign-up, but I was going to get to tryouts no matter what. After four separate telephone calls with Eloise, she talked me into closing my eyes and picking something out of my closet at random. I cheated and only brought my lids to a slit and chose my navy accordian-pleated skirt, and spent the next twenty minutes deciding between my red or my pink turtleneck shirt. I finally chose the red one because I figured there's nothing striking about my shape, and I don't have any outstanding remarkable features, so at least I could wear a striking color.

As I was leaving the house Tuesday morning, my mother gave me instructions. "Maggie, get home as soon as you can. Robby didn't finish his egg and may be coming down with something."

"Mom," I screeched, "tryouts for the Dramatics Club are after school! Tommy can be here!"

"I have to see about some spare parts down at Hanson's garage," Tommy objected, ready for an argument.

"Tommy," my mother told him firmly, "you can come home first and wait for Maggie and then go to Hanson's garage."

I didn't even give Tommy a so-there look. Just an appreciative glance to my mother. At least she hadn't lost her senses about everything.

"When will you be coming home, Mom?"

Tommy asked, insinuating he couldn't depend on my getting there for a year.

"I'll be a little late, because after school I have to go over to Mr. Becker's and give him a copy of the brochure for printing. Daddy and I have decided to use the snapshot Aunt Gretchen took of us last summer in the back yard."

"Not that one, Mom," I protested.

"Honey, you look very nice."

That was just the point.

"Besides, that has a good sharp negative, which he needs."

I grumbled to myself and then to Eloise all the way to school.

"I'm not going to survive this," I told her. "After that scene in the lunchroom, I know I'll turn purple again the second Stevie looks at me in the tryouts."

"You won't."

"I will. I know I will."

"Maybe he won't look at you."

"Thanks."

"He'll look at you, you won't turn purple, and you'll get the lead opposite him. How's that?"

"Not likely."

She finally convinced me to think positive, which I tried. It didn't work too well. Then we arranged where we'd meet after she finished field hockey practice, and after my last class I went to the auditorium.

By the time everybody came, there were about fifteen of us. I noticed Stevie as soon as I walked in. He was leaning against the stage absolutely surrounded by aggressive girls, including Carrie Dean who thinks she owns him. I hate that type. I wish he did, too. Well, at least I didn't have to worry about blushing, since he didn't know I was there. I sat down next to a couple of kids from my class.

Miss Reynolds, the English teacher and drama coach, came in and stood in front of the first row of seats. She held up her arm as a signal for us to get quiet.

"First of all, would the boys who are sitting in another county come down front and join the rest of us?" She looked behind her to the girls who were mobbing Stevie. "You are also invited."

I noticed with special interest that Stevie didn't rush to follow the girls. He sat in the first empty seat he came to.

Miss Reynolds started the session going. "The first play of our theatrical season will be Thornton Wilder's *Our Town*. In the spring, we'll present a musical."

If we last that long, I thought, glumly.

"The essence of *Our Town*," Miss Reynolds was explaining, "is the priceless value of small events in our everyday lives."

That was sure some priceless small event when I fell apart in the lunchroom last week.

"Let's go right along row by row and have you read a few lines. We'll start with Act One, page fourteen, the breakfast scene between Mrs. Gibbs, her son Wally, age sixteen, and her daughter Rebecca, eleven." Miss Reynolds motioned to two girls and a boy.

She handed each of them a copy of the play, and they read the scene where their mother is insisting they finish breakfast, but the kids are in a hurry to leave. I'd seen the play on TV. I liked it, but I thought it was sad because by the end either everyone is dead or the ones who aren't are lonesome for the ones they lost. And the whole thing was that they didn't appreciate them when they were alive. The way things were going right now in my family, there wasn't anyone I could depend on to appreciate. Okay, this morning my mother I could appreciate when she told Tommy off. That was it. Of course, outside the family, Eloise goes without saying. And Stevie—well, considering what my father was plotting, I'd appreciate just seeing him in the corridors for the rest of the year, since nothing else would be left.

Everyone in the first row had read that same scene, and a couple of kids were very good. I mean they really sounded so natural when the girl was objecting to what she was wearing and the boy was wolfing down his food.

"The next scene we'll read is in Act Two, between George and Emily when they are walking home from school." She nodded toward me, since my seat was next. "Maggie, you read Emily on page sixty-two?" She handed me a book and scanned the room for the next boy to do George.

My heart started playing staccato notes. Maybe she'd skip Donald Burgess, who was in my row, and pick Stevie, who was on the end seat in the row behind me.

"Donald Burgess, take the first reading of George."

My heartbeats got back to normal. I gave a passable impression of Emily, and when all fifteen of us had our first run-through, Miss Reynolds called out names of those who should stay to read again and all others could leave. My name was among those to stay, and so, of course, was Stevie's. At least I made the semifinals. So did Carrie Dean.

The next group was getting ready to read from Act Three, where Emily comes back to life. That's a powerful scene that calls for good acting, but I really thought I had the feel for it. Then, just when Miss Reynolds called out the names of the people to read, some boy came in the auditorium and ran down the aisle to the stage.

"Miss Reynolds, I was in the office, and they told me to get Maggie Thayer. She's wanted on the phone."

Me? Who wanted me? What was wrong? Maybe it was a mistake.

"Maggie, you'll have a turn when you come back," Miss Reynolds said that as if to reassure me, since I hadn't moved.

I nodded and walked out, very scared but trying to look nonchalant.

Mr. Sparnock was in the office when I got there.

"Hello, Maggie. You may use the phone on that desk," he showed me which one.

I went over to it and picked it up. "Hello?"

"Maggie!" My brother Tommy shouted in

my ear. I didn't even get a chance to ask what was the matter when he yelled it all out.

"Robby's throwing up all over the place and I don't know where Mom is and I gave up going to the garage and came home early and he's making a mess! A stinking mess and you gotta come right home!"

I smelled it right through the phone and gagged.

"Mom will be home before I can get there," I said, trying to keep my voice low and calm in Mr. Sparnock's hearing.

But calm I didn't feel. Especially since he raved on, "Maggie Thayer, you better come right home or I'll tell Mom you ignored me in an emergency and she might be out for *hours!*"

If only Mr. Sparnock would get out of that office I'd tell my brother a few choice things in a *very loud* voice. But I literally gritted my teeth and said as sweetly as I could and hoped he knew how I really felt, "Of course, Tommy. I'll be right home." I controlled myself again, gently putting the phone back in its cradle instead of banging it down and cracking his head.

"Nothing wrong, I hope, Maggie?" Mr. Sparnock asked me.

"My little brother is sick, and I guess I have to go home."

"I trust it's not serious."

"I don't think so."

He looked at the clock on the wall. "Your mother mentioned she had to go to the printer. She shouldn't be too long."

"I hope not," I said, and headed for the door.

My no-good brother Tommy. All he thinks about is himself. Doesn't matter to him about my interests. . . . I supposed I'd have to go home. Mom might be angry. Oh God, what was that little kid upchucking on? Ugh! I could imagine the stench all over the house and in my bedroom probably. I better go home and air it out.

I went back to the auditorium. Stevie was on the stage with Carrie, reading their lines. What a time for me to have to leave! I *had* to get in that play!

"Everything all right, Maggie?" Miss Reynolds saw me and called from the front of the auditorium.

What did she have to yell it out loud for? Did she want me to yell back so everyone in that room could hear: "My hateful brother called to tell me I should run home and wash the floor my other little brother messed up on?"

I walked down to her and explained quietly.

"I'll arrange for you to have another reading." At least she said that in a normal tone of voice.

"Thanks, Miss Reynolds," I picked up my books from the chair and walked up the aisle, furious with myself for not wearing my pale pink turtleneck. Everyone in Stevie's fan club had to be staring at me in that bright red shirt. What I felt like was one million pieces of a just-finished jigsaw puzzle that somebody deliberately turned upside down on the floor.

Chapter Eight

I was halfway home before I remembered that Eloise would be waiting and wouldn't know what happened to me. I got a case of the sweats trying to make a decision whether I should go back to save Eloise from nervous anxiety or rush home to kill Tommy first.

Revenge won, and I ran the rest of the way. I'd call school and have Eloise paged as soon as Tommy stopped breathing.

"It's about time," he had the gall to snap at me when I opened the door.

"Where did he do it?" I yelled in his face.

"In the john, of course,"

"What do you mean, 'of course'? You told me on the phone he messed up the whole house." I glared at him.

"Well, before he made it to the john he threw up on the floor in the hall upstairs."

"That's all?" I demanded.

"Well, the way he was acting, I got scared," he defended himself, cooling off some.

"One measly barf outside the bathroom and you get hysterical!" I raged at him. "You took me away from a *rehearsal* for a play." I shoved my fist against his chest. "You just wait until I tell Mom. I hope she murders you."

He actually shrank back.

"Did you clean it up?" I bellowed at him.

"Of course."

"Yah, well I'll just go have a look." Before I ran upstairs, I gave him another hard poke, which he didn't try to return. He *knew* how wrong he was.

I looked in Robby's room on the way and saw this puny little face sticking up from his Peanuts pillowcase.

"Hi, Maggie. I was sick." He sounded weak and pitiful.

"But you're okay now, Robby," I said comfortingly.

"I don't know."

"Sure you are."

"I'm glad you're home, Maggie."

It was nice to feel welcomed. I looked down at him and melted.

"See. I was right to call you." Tommy's sneering tone brought back my anger.

"You! You make me *sick!*" I raised my hand threateningly, and he backed away.

"I'm gonna tell Mom!"

"You're lucky I didn't kill you. Get outta my way!" I walked out to the hall to examine the cleanup job when the phone rang.

"Answer that," I ordered.

I kneeled down at the threshold of the john, which took a lot of courage, considering what I expected it to reek of. But Tommy had to see I wasn't going to let him get away with anything less than perfection. Actually it wasn't too bad, but I figured it could stand another scrub.

"You better do this again and make sure it's right this time before Mom gets home."

"Well, do you want me to answer the phone first or not?"

"Answer the phone!" I had a lot of yelling to do to make up for not walloping him.

The bathroom itself didn't have any smell at all. That is, if you don't count that lemon stuff my mother puts in the tank.

"Mom," I told her after the first time she used it, "I'll never be able to eat your lemon meringue pie again as long as I live."

"We'll just use up this container, sweetie; I won't buy any more."

She thought that was an improvement over the fresh mint aroma we had before that.

"It's Eloise . . . for you." I heard Tommy from the cubicle where our upstairs phone is.

I ran over and grabbed it from him. "Beat it."

"Well, I cleaned it up pretty good, didn't I?" He was getting back his usual brashness and I figured I'd quit while I was ahead.

"Okay, scram," I brushed him off. "This is a private call."

"What'd he clean up and what are you doing home?" Eloise sounded agitated.

"I'm home because of my dumb brother. Robby has an upset stomach, and my *dumb brother Tommy* had to call me at school to come home in the middle of tryouts!"

"Oh, Mag. Didn't you get a chance at all?"

"One miserable chance. One. Miss Reynolds said she'd arrange for another reading, but you know who was . . ." I looked around and could see Tommy stalling by the bathroom door. "El, I'll call you back. Nosy here is listening in."

Tommy threw me a scornful look. "Who's interested in what you yak about anyway?"

"You better watch it, fink!" I went downstairs to finish my conversation with Eloise. We made it short.

"Maggie." I heard this tiny little voice coming from upstairs. "Read me a story."

"Sure, honey," I said, starting up the stairs.

"Which book do you want?" I asked when I got to his room.

"Thidwick."

"*Thidwick the Big-Hearted Moose?*"

"That's my favorite."

"It's too sad."

"I don't think it's sad. I think it's funny."

How could he think Thidwick the big-hearted sap was funny? "Are you sure this is the story you want? All about a poor moose who kept letting insects he didn't even know take up housekeeping in his horns, and he was too nice to ask them to leave. That's sad, Robby. When I was five and had tummy upsets, Mommy always used to read me *Ralphie the Pudding Taster*. That's a special story to cure tummyaches."

"Honest?" He looked at me with such belief in his eyes, as if expecting that as soon as I finished the last word of Ralphie, he'd leap out of bed and eat a nine-course dinner. Maybe it would be safer to stick with Thidwick.

It worked out that I didn't have to make a decision.

"Hi, I'm home. How's Robby?"

My mother closed the front door, and I went to the landing.

"He threw up, Mom. But he seems fine now," I called out to her.

Tommy was behind me. "He was real sick, Mom. He really scared me, and I was here all alone."

I gave him a withering look. The sniveling little wretch. He didn't even tell her how come I came home.

"He threw up?" There was anxiety in Mom's voice as she ran up the stairs.

I stayed in there while she checked him out. Then after she took his temp and was satisfied that it was normal, she said it was probably a twenty-four-hour bug and he'd be fine tomorrow.

I really should have killed Tommy. He made me miss finding out if I got the lead or any part in the same play with Stevie. He made me miss just looking at Stevie for at least another half-hour, and I let him get off with only a couple of shoves.

What was the matter with the world anyhow? Two weeks into the eighth grade and everything was working against me. On account of my brothers I'd flunk out of the Dramatics Club, since Miss Reynolds would probably give out all the parts before the day was over. On account of my father going into politics there wouldn't be a dramatic club even if I made the cast, and my social life would be ruined. And my mother, who's supposed to be a girl's best friend, was taking my father's side, and she was welshing on her job, so I had to go home and cover for her.

And what was I doing? Nothing. I was no better than Thidwick—a know-nothing, make-believe, bloodless, gutless *moose*.

Chapter Nine

Anyone standing on our corner watching the cars and people coming out and going in my house would have thought we were running some kind of clinic. Besides the traffic outside there were the phone calls inside. As soon as my mother or father finished one, the phone rang again. In less than one week since Dad had been asked to be a candidate, Mom had gotten committees formed, made arrangements for evaluations and strategy meetings, and the family room was now the unofficial campaign headquarters for Hal Thayer. Tommy was behaving in his usual frenzied way, working on "promotion." Daddy made a speech to the Ward Three Undecideds, and everyone but me was moving ahead in high gear.

When I came into school the next morning, Miss Randall asked me if Friday in C Block would be okay for me to work with Doreen.

Whatever she said.

"One day next week all the aides and faculty advisers will meet to talk over everyone's experiences."

"That'll be fine."

She gave me an approving smile and then remembered to tell me, "Miss Reynolds would like you to stop in her room when you have a chance."

My heart pounded and my cheeks felt hot. "Can I go now, Miss Randall, and get back here before the bell? Okay?"

She looked at the wall clock. "Sure. You can make it."

I flew out of there and four doors down the hall to one-seventeen. On the door was her sign: Ellen Reynolds, English.

"Hi, Miss Reynolds."

"Good morning, Maggie. I hope your brother is all better."

"Oh, he's fine."

"Your parents are pretty busy these days with the election, I understand."

I wish she'd stop beating around the bush and get to the point. When was I getting a reading?

"They sure are. It's wild around our house."

"There's a great deal involved in campaigning. I'm sure if your father wins it will be worth all the hard work."

"Yeah. Sure."

I wondered if she knew she'd probably lose her job if my father got elected. Did she know what his platform was? If she did, I'd never get chosen for the play.

"Maggie, I'd like to have you run through a couple of scenes, and I want Shirley Prentice to read again, also."

She didn't mention Carrie Dean. Did that mean she was eliminated? Or did she get the part of Emily? I'll die if she did.

"Steve Garber and John Gorley will be doing

either Wally or George, so the four of you will be auditioning together."

She did say Steve Garber. My life just turned over a new leaf. I am born again.

"During C Block on Friday seems to be a convenient time for the group and me. Can you make it? I see that you have a free period then."

"Ohhhhh."

"Something wrong?"

Born again? I just died.

"I have to be a tutor aide during my C Block free period Friday."

"Well, let's see. . . . How about Friday after school?"

She'd get them to switch!

She went on talking. "I could read the parts of the other characters and make the decision at that time. Or," she got another idea, "perhaps Shirley can come after school and read with you."

Big thrill. Shirley wasn't the one I wanted to read with. But I couldn't hold anything against Miss Reynolds; she was trying. Actually, I couldn't have anything against Doreen for C Block either. She didn't make the plan.

"Friday after school will be okay," I said. But it wasn't really. If I could have read Emily in that tender scene while Stevie did George, Miss Reynolds would see what a beautiful, natural blend we were. . . . Well, I had to get back to my homeroom.

"I'll meet you in the auditorium, Maggie, right after the bell on Friday."

"I'll be there."

At lunch Gail and Debbie were talking about program cuts like it was a continuation from where they left off the day before. Debbie said her mother was building up the great winter climate in Florida and saying how Debbie could have a fabulous year-round tan, and Gail sounded like she could use a sedative when she told us her parents were considering private school if any changes were made in the Oakdale system.

"I told them I would commit suicide if they took me out of W.W."

"Did that shake them up?" Eloise asked her.

"Not exactly. My father started describing how you can find the exact place in your neck if you wanted to slit your throat and there'd be instant death and not much of a bloody mess."

"Where is it?" Debbie was feeling her throat and looking interested. "It might convince my mother. If I let her think I knew how to do it she'd quit threatening me."

"Ha-ha."

"Ha-ha yourself."

Then we all sighed in unison on account of our own particular troubles, and somebody said how great it was going to be when we'd be on our own and no one would be dictating to us or interfering in our lives in any way.

I was just getting out of my last-period French class when I saw Doreen.

"Hi, Doreen." I knew I didn't have to tell her who I was.

She stopped, and her face got that lit-up look. "Hi, Maggie. Miss Randall said we'd meet Friday in C Block. I'm so glad."

"Me, too." I hoped it sounded sincere. I didn't want to hurt her feelings. I mean, she didn't know what I was giving up.

"I was going to call you up tonight to find out if you could come over to my house tomorrow after school."

"Oh." That really took me by surprise, and I didn't know what to say.

"We don't have to read. . . . I mean, we could just have some fun, okay?"

How could I refuse her? I don't mean that I didn't want to go, but I wasn't sure what it would be like.

"You could go home with me in the station wagon. You know, the one that takes me and the others to school and back every day."

"That'd be great." I tried to let her feel I was enthusiastic. "Where do you live?"

"On Martin Road. Do you know where that is?"

"That's way the other side of town, isn't it?"

Oh, boy. That sounded as if I meant it was a crummy section. I didn't and it wasn't, but it got said and I wasn't going to make it worse by working at an explanation.

"It's not too far. My mother said you could catch the five-ten bus home. It leaves from the corner of our street and goes near where you live."

"Neat." I agreed to meet her in her home-room right after school the next day.

Eloise stayed for field hockey practice again, and there was no real incentive for me to watch, since I haven't mastered the rules of the game. I walked home with some other girls, and when I got to our driveway I saw two cars parked there that I didn't recognize. My mother must have left school the second the bell rang to get started on one of her committee meetings.

Shirking her job like that. I wondered how much Mrs. Williams, the principal, was going to put up with. I could see the whole picture: my mother would be out of work; then she'd have more time to bring the campaign to a successful conclusion; my father would get elected; Gail would go to private school; Debbie would go to Florida; and Eloise and I would find the right place in our necks to cut our throats with a mini-mum of blood loss, but certain death would result.

I was right. I hardly made it inside when I heard the buzz from downstairs.

"Terry, I think the letters should be in heavy type—more prominent."

"Do you think we ought to take this back to Mr. Becker?"

"Lorrie, we need a price on that."

"Millie, can Walter get this to the newspaper by tomorrow?"

I escaped into the kitchen, dumped my

books, and headed for the fridge. Not one interesting thing in there to tempt anybody's palate. Well, no matter how the election came out, at least if my mother got fired she would have more time for getting food in the house.

I tried the freezer. In between the frozen meat packages was one mutilated container of ice cream. Tommy's work, no doubt. I pulled the top off to find about two tablespoons of sorry-looking pistachio. Tommy's favorite flavor.

I opened the cookie jar. Empty.

This place was falling apart. Maybe I should sign up for the gourmet cooking class. What was I thinking! Sign up? Hah.

My mother at that very moment was working her head off to make sure there would be nothing to sign up for in the entire community of Oakdale.

Later, when the committee went home, I didn't even bother mentioning to her how she was neglecting her children and jeopardizing her career. I just didn't have any fight in me. I felt like Thidwick all over again.

Chapter Ten

If someone told me before I started being a tutor aide that I was going to have to ride in the station wagon with four handicapped kids, I would have had an upset stomach for a week and looked out the window at the scenery for the whole trip. It turned out it didn't faze me at all, and Joey was even one of the boys in there.

"Hi, M-M-Mag-gie." He made those sounds as soon as he saw me get in the wagon. I knew what he said all right. To me it was clear as day. He remembered me and my name after more than a whole summer being away. There was nothing wrong with *his* brain.

The two others had petit mal, which I now know is the same as mild seizures. That sounds worse than it must be, because I've never seen either of those kids have any fits.

I didn't try to figure out why I wasn't bothered until later on, when I was riding home on the bus. The best reason I came up with was what Mrs. Hall had said in her orientation speech—that if you haven't been exposed to things like that or had close contact with it, then you really don't know what it's all about.

Doreen's was the third stop, about twenty minutes after we got started. Her house is in what you'd call a development, since every house on both sides of the street looks the same except for the colors. They all have little patches of lawn in front of these one-story cottages and a driveway with a separate one-car garage. Doreen's mother was standing outside a yellow house with white shutters, waving and grinning. Just as if Doreen could see her.

She ran to her mother in a straight line from the car as if the path was laid out in Braille. "This is Maggie." The way she said my name it could have been "Her Majesty the queen." It embarrassed me, but it also made me feel good in an unusual way.

Mrs. Marshall told me how glad she was to see me and that we should go in the kitchen and take cold root beer and a piece of warm, right-out-of-the-oven gingerbread. I thought of our empty cookie jar as I lapped up every crumb.

When we got through, Doreen took the plates and glasses over to the sink and washed them. I wondered how she could tell if they were clean.

"Where's the dish towel?" I offered to wipe.

"Under the sink right in front of me." She backed away so I could open the cabinet door. "Pull out the rack. There should be a dry one hanging."

There was.

When I picked up each dish I noticed they were spotless, and when we finished, she put everything back where it looked like it belonged.

"We can go in my room and see what we feel like doing."

Her room was down a narrow hall. The windows faced the back yard, which had mostly lawn but with a couple of evergreen bushes and a maple tree. It was a pretty view. What difference did it make to Doreen, though, what the view was?

We felt the warm breeze from her open window. Nobody was in the yard, and we could hear a bird in the maple tree. We stood for a few seconds listening, and when he flew away she said, "I love being here by myself when it's real quiet and I sort of tune in to the outside sounds. Sometimes what you hear is like music."

Maybe, being blind, she was forced to find different kinds of things to enjoy than if she could see. I mean, who ever stands in front of an open window just to listen to birds?

When we were through looking out the window, my eyes drifted over to the wall, and a big *"Wow"* came out of my mouth. I don't know how come I didn't notice that first, because when you come into Doreen's room, the thing that has to hit you right off is her wallpaper. It's this wet-look vinyl. I mean, it is *bright.* Swirls of color. The whole wall beside her bed is a mass of red, orange, aqua, and violet in a swirly-swirly pattern.

After my "wow," she laughed and said, "Pretty wild paper, right?"

I thought, I could walk into a room and she'd probably tell me what color dress I was wearing or where my jeans were faded. I wanted to ask her how she knew what I was looking at, but I didn't dare.

Then she added, as if to explain, "Everyone who sees it for the first time comes out with a 'wow' like that."

I felt sad when she said it. That meant she had to go by other people's reactions and had to take certain things on their say-so.

"Is there anything special you'd like to do, Maggie?"

"What do you usually do?"

"Oh, I listen to records or ride my bike or—"

"Ride your bike?" The picture of her doing that came before me. Weird.

"Yes, but I don't think we could today." She said it matter-of-factly. "Unless Jeff isn't going to use his and if you don't mind riding a boy's bike."

I didn't mind riding a boy's bike. That didn't seem to me to be the point. It was one thing to wash dishes and know if doorways had wide openings and even sense when certain people came in the room, but riding a bike! In traffic!

"We could play Monopoly until Jeffie gets home, and then I could ask him."

How could she play Monopoly? But still, she made the suggestion.

She took out the board and everything and set it on the floor. We sat down, and as she took out the cards I could see that all of them had Braille tabs on the corners. I noticed the rest of the game and saw that the board and play money were marked in the same way.

We were concentrating on who was going to buy Park Place when I heard, "Hi, Dorrie."

I looked up to see a boy, who of course was her brother Jeff. He looked a lot like her. He was nice-looking in the same way she was pretty, but there was no question about his eyes. He could see, all right. The big difference between his and Doreen's was like the difference between a blank expression and a wide-open, alive look.

"Hi, Jeff. This is Maggie. Maggie, this is my brother Jeff."

I didn't think I'd be able to carry off an introduction like that if she came to my house. I'd probably forget my own brother's name.

Jeff said, "Hi, Maggie," and I barely whispered a "hi."

"Jeffie, if you're not going to ride your bike, could Maggie use it?"

He scratched his head like he was giving it his consideration. Maybe he had to figure how he was going to shuffle around his schedule. He reminded me of Tommy that way.

"Well, I was going over to Dicky Cranston's with my stamp collection, but I suppose I can walk there."

The resemblance between him and Tommy just ended. I couldn't quite picture my brother doing anything like that for me. Well, I suppose Jeff had to be especially nice to Doreen, under the circumstances. But my blood was pumping down to my fingertips. . . . How was I going to ride with her? I mean, how could she get around on a bike?

So I got a brainstorm and looked at my watch. The bus left at five-ten, and Mom had said be sure to leave enough time to catch it. It was four-thirty. Maybe I could say it was getting late. I tried it.

"We have time, Maggie. It takes only a minute to get to the bus."

"Don't forget to put it back when you get through, Doreen," Jeff said. "Last time I let you borrow it, it didn't turn up until a day later."

That sounded more like home.

"Jeff Marshall, you know why. That was when Judy's bike was being repaired and it started to pour and your bike was the fastest way for her to get back to her house." Doreen looked mad for the first time since I'd met her.

"If it starts to pour this afternoon, I promise not to ride back to my house on your bike, Jeff," I broke in, in case it got to be a fight.

"Okay, that's a promise." He gave me a see-that-you-do look.

I just smiled and had a more comfortable feeling that they were like a normal family.

Jeff left, and Doreen said with exasperation, "Brothers! Do you have any?"

"Two. Robby is only six, and he's okay, but Tommy is eleven and can be a real pest."

I wanted so much to know how come she was blind and Jeff wasn't, and if that bothered her. I didn't ask.

I helped her pick up the Monopoly pieces, and she put them all back in the box carefully. I wondered if she naturally had patience or if she learned to be that way by necessity.

She called to her mother on the way out and told her what we were going to do.

"Fine, girls. Come back in plenty of time for Maggie's bus."

We went outside, and my heart moved into my throat when we got on those bikes.

"We can ride to the bus stop, Maggie, so you-can see where it is, if you like."

"Sh-sure."

"The only thing you have to remember about biking with me is you have to stay right beside me. Real close to the right-hand sidewalk. It's not like I use my cane on the bike." She laughed.

I heard myself make a small nervous laugh at what she said. Not because I thought it was funny.

We rode down the driveway to the street, and her mother waved to us. "Have fun." She smiled and didn't look the least bit worried. She didn't even say "Be careful," the way mothers do.

"We go left here for two blocks, and the bus stop where you get on is on the right side of the street."

Fortunately for both of us there was no traffic. After the bus stop she said we could just ride around and make a loop back to her house, coming up from the other end of the development. There were about twenty streets, half of them dead ends or little circular paths with houses about twenty-five feet apart. I could see then that, the way the place was laid out, for her to ride a bike wasn't as impossible as it had seemed to be before. Once, some kids were at a corner ready to cross, and I tooted my horn so they'd wait. I didn't know if I should have made the announcement to Doreen in advance or not. I didn't, and she didn't ask. Later, two or three cars came toward us on a couple of streets, but since we were on the right side of the road it worked out all right. But for the first five minutes at least, I was pretty paralyzed with fright. I got over that when I realized Doreen was chattering away, totally relaxed. Well, if *she* wasn't scared, I guessed I certainly had no right to be.

I wondered if she had any other friends. With a handicap like hers, I couldn't imagine she'd be the most popular kid on the block. I asked her about Judy, the girl she mentioned who borrowed Jeff's bike.

"She's new here. She just moved in, down the street."

"Are there many girls your age in the neighborhood?"

"There may be, but I don't know any of them."

I guessed I hadn't been too subtle. I decided I wouldn't push the subject, but she was explaining.

"I didn't get to meet anyone from around here because I was at Kingsley—you know, the school for the blind."

I winced when she said that. I said. "It's nice that you know Judy now."

"Yes, but of course she doesn't know anyone else yet. You're the only one who . . . I mean you and Judy are the only ones I know in Oakdale."

That gave me a funny feeling. The way she hesitated, was she going to say Judy and I were the only ones she knew who weren't blind? I wondered if she wanted to be friends with me only because I could see, or did she like me for myself? She had turned her face to me and smiled when she said that, though. I wanted to believe she meant it.

It was just five o'clock when we put the bikes back in the garage and went back in her house.

"Okay if I walk Maggie to the bus, Mummy?"

"Of course, dear." Mrs. Marshall came over to us. "It was lovely of you to come, Maggie. You must visit us again when you can." She took my hands between hers. It was as loving as a hug.

"I'd like that," I said. I didn't even have the sense to ask if Doreen could come to my house.

She went right on as if I'd said something real nice. "We're all so pleased you are Doreen's social studies reader." Then she frowned away her happy expression like she suddenly thought of something disturbing. "We certainly hope the city won't have to lay off teachers in the special education program."

I felt my insides turn cold. "Did you hear they were going to do that, Mrs. Marshall?"

"There have been rumors. I know cuts will be made, but it would be very hard for us if we had to give up the excellent facilities at Woodrow Wilson. And the music program. Doreen has started piano at school. She was in the advanced class at Kingsley and—"

"Oh, Mummy!"

Doreen acted like any kid who'd be embarrassed by her mother praising her in front of someone, but I thought, in this case, I could understand Mrs. Marshall looking for anything that Doreen did, even if it was only average, and want to brag about it.

I was dying to tell her I didn't want my programs cut either. None of the kids did. I wanted to say that only a monster would take away any of those excellent facilities. But how could I say one word? I couldn't let on that my father probably thought all that equipment in the resource room was nothing but frills and money wasters and that music was no more basic than dramatics.

Mrs. Marshall gave me a smiling good-bye, and I did my best to do the same.

Doreen took her cane, naturally, to guide her along the sidewalks. I was so unused to the idea of someone being blind that the procedures she used to get around seemed like secret rites. After we crossed the first intersection, I got nerve enough to bring up what was bothering me.

"What your mother said, Doreen, about—about laying off—like Miss Sheehan—what would you do?"

"I don't know." There was worry in her voice. "My father says that even if they let a lot of the regular teachers go, the classes would get overcrowded, and he thinks it would be harder for me to learn. I'd hate to go back to that private school. I'd have to live there, and I wouldn't like that. Particularly after being in a . . . a regular school."

That was all we said while we waited for the bus. Then when it came we said good-bye about ten times until I got on. I found a window seat, and both of us kept waving, but somehow I didn't have to wonder if she knew I was doing it, too.

Chapter Eleven

Only a monster would take away the resource room or the music program. I thought that over and over all the way home. My father was no way a monster, so that plan couldn't possibly be in his mind. Could it be that he was so anxious to be elected that he'd *compromise* his *integrity?* No. Not my dad.

At supper that night I waited for a break in what was now the only topic discussed at the table. Being at Doreen's that afternoon made me realize how much more important the special education and music programs were to Doreen than the Dramatics Club and the athletic teams were to me and Eloise. Not that we didn't feel it as much, but for Doreen's actual needs, there was no comparison.

Somewhere between calves' liver (yecch) and chocolate pudding (tasteless, since Mom didn't have time to make her own) everyone must have been chewing at the same time, and I got my chance.

"Uh, Dad, today I was visiting the girl I've been reading to—the blind girl . . ."

He swallowed a mouthful and gave me his nicest smile. "Do you realize that she could get an A in that course because of you?"

A perfect lead-in!

"If she gets an A, Dad, it will be because of the wonderful things in the resource room. You know that room, don't you?"

"I haven't seen it, but I've been told of the excellent materials there."

I had it made! "Then you certainly approve of it, right?"

"I certainly do."

I quickly made my point while I had the advantage. "Then that wouldn't be included in any cuts, would it?"

"It depends on how you look at it, honey. You see, fortunately there are very few school-age children in Oakdale who are blind." He stopped and looked toward the kitchen where the phone had just rung.

"I'll get it," Mom said.

Then Daddy went on with his ominous remarks. "That's one of the problems we have to work out. Can we afford to maintain faculty—"

"Hal, dear"—Mom came back into the dining room—"Ken Berns says it's vital to talk to you right now."

Daddy patted my hand and went into the kitchen. I got up and listlessly took some plates off the table. So much for having it made.

I never got a chance to call Eloise that night because my parents monopolized the phone. I figured I'd talk to her on the way to school about being at Doreen's. But the next morning she was worked up about her soccer, and I couldn't barge in on her with another subject.

"Ruth Thomas thinks she's going to beat me

out for center forward on the soccer team. What do you think about her nerve?"

She was waiting for me to answer her question.

"Well, how about that, Mag? Does she have nerve or doesn't she?"

"Yeah."

I could feel her giving me a puzzled stare. "Whaddaya mean, 'yeah'? What kind of talk is that? My reputation is on the line, and all you can say is 'yeah'?"

Gail and Debbie had caught up with us, and I didn't find an opening in the conversation to explain that my mind wasn't on what she was saying.

Why did some people have it so tough? Wasn't it bad enough that Doreen couldn't see? Now there was this threat hovering over her that all this great new life at a regular school was going to be snatched away. It was so crazy unfair that to look on the good side would be to wish there were more blind kids in Oakdale so it would be financially worthwhile to keep Miss Sheehan.

Eloise and I didn't have the same lunch period that day, so I still didn't get to talk to her, and it was already C Block.

As soon as I got to room two-twelve, Doreen said, "Jeff told me to be sure to say thanks for returning his bike and any time you want to use it again, he'll consider it."

"Oh, he will, will he? Tell him I appreciate that. But he better hope it won't rain the next time I use it. You never can tell when I'd return it."

We both laughed. "Do you think you *could* come again, Maggie?"

If her eyes had had any life in them I know how they would have looked when she asked me that. I was ashamed of myself for thinking she liked me only because I wasn't blind. And then it recklessly spilled out of me. "Doreen, weren't you ever able to see? Ever?"

She held her head in the same position, not moving or even blinking. "I was okay when I was born, but I didn't weigh enough, so they put me in an incubator. It had something to do with too much oxygen."

I made myself ask it. "How come Jeff wasn't . . ."

"He weighed enough." Just like that.

I felt I should say something—something important. But I didn't know what.

There was an awful silence. After a bit she asked me, "Do you know John Rossman?"

The name sounded familiar. I wasn't sure.

"He's here at Woodrow Wilson. He's in a wheelchair."

Oh, yes. Mr. Kahn had mentioned him to Harvey the day we had orientation. "I don't know him, but Harvey Ferris helps him with math," I said.

"You know what Johnny wants more than anything?"

No, I didn't. "What?"

"Well, the thing he wants most, he can never have. That's to be a professional basketball player."

How would she know that? Those handicapped kids must get together. Like a club, maybe. All the rest of us have never gotten that close to them, we hardly even know their names, let alone what they want most in the world. For a second I felt kind of left out. A bunch of kids get together and don't invite me in. Hey, that was funny, wasn't it? We always thought it was the other way around—we didn't want *them* in.

"You should see him throw baskets, Maggie," she continued. "He just sits there in his wheelchair, and—oh, easy—he makes a basket every time!"

What was she telling me? I should "see" him. I mean, how did she know it was so easy?

"You remember Pamela Walden, Maggie? She was one of the girls in the station wagon yesterday."

She was one of those who had epilepsy that you'd never know anything was wrong with unless she got an attack. Yeah, I remembered.

"Her mother got permission to use the gym for her birthday party, and we all came—and that's when Johnny Rossman was making those baskets." She had this big admiration in her voice.

We all came. . . . She must have meant all the seventeen handicapped kids who go to Woodrow Wilson.

"He was making even more baskets than Danny Cavelletti. I mean it."

"How come Danny Cavelletti was there? I thought you meant only the—I mean just . . ." Oh, boy, I put my foot where my mouth is, all right.

"Danny was practicing in the gym when we got there, and Johnny asked him to stay awhile." She said it as easily as if I hadn't made any booboo at all.

I was wondering what made her bring up John Rossman's name when she said, "Maggie, you know, people don't feel the same about everyone who has a handicap. It depends on what kind of a handicap it is."

"Yes, I . . . I guess that's right."

"The thing with Johnny is, he can't walk—but nobody thinks his brain is affected. But if you're blind"—her voice was getting angry—"everyone thinks you can't do anything. You're supposed to bump into furniture; you can't go out alone or you'll get yourself killed; you are just plain stupid!"

And I had thought she was pretty casual about her problem. She cared, all right. But it looked like she cared even more that people thought her stupid on account of her blindness, than she was upset over the blindness itself.

"But if people know you, Doreen, they don't feel that way."

"They don't let you give them a chance to get that far."

I wanted to say, "But I have." I couldn't, though, because it wouldn't have been honest. If I hadn't been trapped into getting to know her, I'd have still been stuck in the same rut as all those others.

I was desperate to find something hopeful to tell her. "Maybe things will get better now that we have this program here. I mean, we don't know for *sure* they're going to get rid of it." That was a deceitful thing to say. It was like I was holding out juicy plums that were going to turn into dried-out prunes. I got chills down my spine starting at the back of my neck, and my feelings came pouring out of me. "Everything *has to stay the same*. Then more kids here will have the chance to get to know you, Doreen, like I have!"

There, I said it, and that was true. The program *had* to stay! But how?

Chapter Twelve

In French, my last-period class, I had trouble translating, thinking of Doreen. Madame Beauvais raised her eyebrows at me in surprise.

"Marguerite!"

She uses the most French-sounding pronunciation she can dredge up for everyone's name. Like we've got a boy in our class whose family just came from Puerto Rico and his name is Pedro. She calls him Pierre.

"Marguerite, *vous êtes malade aujourd'hui?*" Which in case you don't get it, reads, "Maggie, you sick today?" I was, in a way.

The last bell rang, and Eloise stuck her head in the door. "Meet me in the gym after your audition, Mag."

Audition? What audi . . . oh, *no!* My head really was in separate pieces. How could I forget that? But actually, even if my mind was on it I don't expect I'd have been foaming at the mouth with excitement over Shirley Prentice substituting for Stevie.

My face must have shown the confusion I was feeling, only Eloise didn't interpret it right. She gave me a slow smile like she understood how tensed up I was about getting the part. She said, "Hey, Mag, you're a shoo-in for the part of Emily."

I smiled back and nodded, appreciating Eloise very much. How would she know I was confused for a totally different reason. I'd explain it to her later.

"Yuh, I'll give it my all, Eloise."

Walking to the auditorium I knew I had to forget Doreen temporarily and focus my mind on reading the play. Even if Miss Reynolds or Shirley acted the part of George, I would pretend while I was doing the lines that Stevie was going to be reading George back to me. If I pretended that, it would be easy, because Emily's feelings were very similar to mine. Of course this was supposed to take place around eighty years ago, but I think, basically, people's *feelings* for each other are pretty much the same now as they used to be. I mean, even from Shakespeare's day, like Romeo and Juliet, or Elizabeth Barrett Browning—those love poems she wrote to her husband . . . I could easily identify with her.

The auditorium was empty when I got there. Did I make a mistake? I remembered distinctly she said Friday right after the last bell. My feet were kind of hesitating as I walked toward the stage.

"I see you're more prompt than I am, Maggie." I heard her voice behind me.

I looked around, and my blood pressure shot up like a rocket through the roof. Stevie was walking beside her. I was either dreaming or had just lost my mind. Either way, I was numb.

"I just happened to run into Steve, here, who will be George in the play, and he said he'd be glad to read opposite you today, Maggie."

He'd be glad! My eyes darted over to him. He had a real teasing look and said, "Actually, I put up quite a struggle, but she bribed me that I'd get the part of George, so I said I'd do it." Then he pursed his lips keeping back a smile so there shouldn't be any mistake that he was kidding.

I tried to appear cool. I really wanted to make some crack back, jokingly, like "Sure, everyone knows that's the only way you'd get the part," but I couldn't. I managed a smile, at least, the kind that let him know I didn't take him seriously, but what I brilliantly said was, "Gee, thanks, Stevie. That was real nice of you."

He swung his hand in a think-nothing-of-it gesture, and I turned around so I wouldn't be walking backward to the stage.

Miss Reynolds said, handing both of us copies of *Our Town*, "Page sixty-one middle of page, George's line. Steve, you begin with 'Can I carry.'"

He's asking if he can carry Emily's books home from school. She's supposed to be toughed up because he hasn't been noticing her lately, and she's giving him the impression she could care less as she says, "Thank you." The directions are that she looks at him while she says it.

My eyes were glued to the page. My head was even bowed, facing my knees. I whispered, "Thank you," like I needed a shot of adrenaline to stay alive. Stevie, as George, comes right in on that saying, "Excuse me." Only Stevie didn't. He just stood there like he was waiting for me to say my line. He must not have heard me.

I made a nervous, shaky sigh and said the

line again, louder. It came out a shriek and it scared me. I managed to look at him so he'd know I was through and waiting for my next cue from him.

The scene then moves into the drugstore where they have a soda and he tells her he's giving up college so he can be close to her. That's the one filled with all that emotion that really grabs you. The one I knew I could handle like a charm. In my mind, that is. In actual life it didn't happen.

After the audition was over, Miss Reynolds said, "Thank you, Steve. There's a scene between Rebecca and Mrs. Gibbs that I want to run through with you, Maggie. Can you stay for another few minutes?"

I said yes, but I realistically had no expectations that I'd get picked for anything, except maybe stagehand, where I'd set the furniture in the right places.

I heard Stevie say, "Good luck," as he was leaving. I swallowed the lump in my throat, and it landed in my chest as if it was going to settle there permanently, and I muttered, "Thanks, I'll need it."

"Maggie, let's take it from page fourteen. You read the line that starts with 'Don't make a noise,' " Miss Reynolds instructed me.

I turned to page fourteen and found the place. It's Mrs. Gibbs's line, and she's talking to Rebecca, her daughter.

"You want me to read her line? You mean the next line, Rebecca's." I said it like I knew she had looked at the wrong speech by mistake.

"No, I'd like to hear you do Mrs. Gibbs. She has a good, strong role, Maggie."

That "good, strong role" was George's mother. How could I play George's mother who would be, in the play, Stevie's mother! If I couldn't be Emily, his girl friend and later his *wife*, then I wasn't interested in being *in* the stupid play.

"Carrie going to be Emily?" The inside of my mouth felt as if it had been stranded on the desert for six weeks.

"No, I haven't chosen anyone for Emily yet. But I'd like to hear *you* in Mrs. Gibbs's part."

Putting the emphasis on *you* in Mrs. Gibbs's part was obvious. She was taking pity on me because the way I was performing, anyone would take pity on me.

So I read Mrs. Gibbs. I didn't feel like Mrs. Gibbs. I didn't put my heart in the reading, and the big result was that I didn't get the part . . . any part. Stage manager, either.

I left the auditorium feeling sick, knowing I had just lost my last chance for the year or forever to make that meaningful relationship with Stevie Garber. I started walking toward the gym, slowly, the way you'd do if you were in a trance. So I didn't notice him at first. To me it was just a figure walking down the corridor. Then I saw it was Stevie.

"How did it go?" he asked me.

"Not too well," I murmured. I mean, he *knew* how awful I was.

"That's too bad," he said.

"Well, yeah, I'm just a rotten actress."

"Oh, I don't know."

"You ought to," I heard myself say and was surprised.

He made a kind of smile I'll remember all my life.

"You can try again for the spring play," he said encouragingly.

"If there is one." My tongue jumped ahead of my thoughts, and it sounded irritable. I certainly didn't want to sound that way to him. But after all, he couldn't be too optimistic about the outcome either, knowing the power that my father was wielding.

"I try not to think about it."

I was right. "If they do cut dramatics, that'll be awful for you, won't it? I mean that's important to you."

"It sure is. That's what I'm hoping to get some college scholarship money in—if I can."

Listening to him, I thought again how much having a program means to people who are serious about it. I mean, for me, Dramatics Club meant only being near Stevie. But for him and anyone else who was planning for a career in it, it was vital. It mattered the same to them as the resource room and music program mattered to Doreen.

"I hope they keep it, Stevie, for your sake." My voice almost shook from the emotion I felt. He looked at me like he knew I meant it.

"Thanks," he said. "That's real nice of you." Which was quite a different way than I had said the same words to him a little while before.

We stood there for a second, saying nothing more. That was a very special moment. Then he gave his pile of books a hitch. "Well, see ya." He smiled.

"Yeah." I nodded, and then we turned in opposite directions and took off.

I walked on air down the hallway. If Stevie Garber was a very ordinary looking boy with zits all over his face, in my eyes he would still be the most gorgeous boy in the whole world.

Chapter Thirteen

I handled that dialogue between Stevie and me without stumbling once. I did it better than when I was trying to be an actress. How did that happen? Wait'll I tell Eloise! I doubled up my speed and whizzed down the corridor.

I pushed open the gym door and almost tripped over my own feet. There wasn't a sound in the room.

"Eloise, Eloise," I called out wildly. My voice echoed and bounced off the wall.

Miss Henderson, our gym teacher, who was at the oppostie end of the gym, started yelling instructions, and about six girls ran toward a soccer ball that was rolling on the floor. Eloise was just about to get a good toehold on it when Ruth Thomas appeared, like out of the woodwork, and gave it a hard kick, making it fly across the gym. Then there was a big scramble while the whole team started running around like crazy and making all kinds of athletic noises. Even if my voice pierced Eloise's eardrum she wouldn't have heard it at the time like that. I'd just have to control myself and save it until she was through.

I squatted, ready to sit on the floor and wait, when the ball got kicked in my direction and I figured I'd better get out of there before I got killed. I squeezed against the wall, moving sideways avoiding the sweaty bodies. Every one of them charged in eight directions in the course of a few seconds, and in between their grunts and screams I heard Eloise's voice.

"See you in ten minutes, Mag," she said breathlessly. Then she and the rest of them were off playing in another corner.

"Okay," I yelled back. I honestly didn't see what she got out of that stuff.

As I waited out there in the hall, every single syllable came back to me. I heard the tone of his voice, saw his face, his dark hair, his eyes, his cheekbones—the kind that show, that give character to a face. I've always admired the cheekbone type. Mine are covered with flesh. I'm not fat, but my face is the kind that if you look at it and not the rest of my body, you'd figure me for a hippo. Well, almost.

I went over the whole episode, word for word. What did he say exactly? Well, he asked me if I got the part. . . . No, that wasn't it. He told me how disappointed he was. . . . No, not precisely. Well, he *did talk* to me! And he gave me a meaningful look!

"I hope they cut the whole entire and total sports program from every school in Oakdale and Miss Henderson is the first one to get the ax!" Eloise's angry voice brought me out of my reverie.

She was standing in front of me in her gym shorts and T-shirt, her arms folded across her chest. I knew without her telling me: Ruth Thomas got center forward position, which Eloise wanted and thought she was better qualified for.

"Oh, I'm sorry, El."

She had misery written all over her face. Her upper lip was being held in check by her front teeth, but her power to keep it stiff seemed uncertain. Maybe my being sympathetic wasn't what she needed.

"Hey, we're both in the same boat, buddy. I just got released from the Woodrow Wilson Dramatic Club, probably for all time."

"We're both losers, Mag."

What could I say? "Oh, I'm no loser—Stevie just talked to me"? I mean, so what? But on the other hand, she hadn't lost everything; she'd still be on the team. No matter how low her position was, she wouldn't quit.

I meekly told her so, hoping she'd see it that way.

"Quit?" She said it like it was shot out of her like a bullet. "There was only one position left to play, and Ruth got it. I'm out, Mag. You understand? *Out!*"

I grabbed her arm with my free hand. I could have cried for her, but all I could say in a sad voice was "Eloise."

She unfolded her arms and pressed my hand.

We were the only ones in the hallway. It was quiet and late enough in the day so that we might have been the only two people left in the building—except for the members of the girls' soccer team, who were taking showers and changing into their street clothes. But the locker room was far enough away so we couldn't even hear any muffled, distant sounds. Somehow the stillness seemed magnified because we weren't rushing with words the way we always do.

And then, maybe because of the silence or my depressed feeling, my thoughts went back to Doreen. Her needs were the most important. Eloise could major in athletics in college, and Stevie could work on his acting in high school. But Doreen was *now!*

"Eloise, we've got to *do* something!"

"Like what? You think I should murder Miss Henderson and you should murder Miss Reynolds?"

"That's not what I mean, El. We've got to help Doreen."

She scowled and said, losing her temper, "Aren't you helping her enough, reading to her and all? And what am I supposed to do for her? Besides what does she have to do with what's happened to us? Whose best friend are you anyway?"

I never heard her sound like that before. But I knew she was uptight only on account of the soccer thing. So I didn't yell back at her. I told her in a regular voice, but with a lot of feeling so she wouldn't have any doubts, "*You* are my best friend and always will be, and you're the only one I'd talk to like this. You're the one I can count on to help."

Her face muscles relaxed a little.

"El, there's a lot I haven't had a chance to tell you. I was over at Doreen's house yesterday; she asked me to come. Her mother was telling me how great Doreen plays the piano, and they're afraid all the services she's getting, like piano lessons, will be cut and she—she—El, she's *blind!*"

I knew I'd said it as if it was a new piece of information, but all I meant was, now that I knew from what Doreen herself *told* me how messed up her life was, I felt like it was up to people like us to help her.

I think that sobered Eloise. I mean, it sank through to her. She was nodding, like she understood what I was talking about, not angry.

"You mean we won't be busy with extracurricular activities, so we'll have time to work on something."

"I mean it doesn't make any difference if we have our own extracurricular things or not."

By the time we got to the locker room I had filled her in about Doreen. Not only that she'd have to go back to her old boarding school if the cuts went through, but how she felt when everybody figured her for being helpless just because she was blind.

"You get that, El? *Just* because she's blind. That's how she looks at it . . . if you'll excuse the expression."

"Yeah, yeah," she repeated catching on to the whole thing.

Both of us squeezed into her locker, and I sat on the bench.

"So what *will* we do, El?"

My question just hung there without an answer all the time she changed her clothes and squashed her gym stuff into a paper bag. She was punching it as if the uniform was responsible for her not playing better. She gave it one last poke and looked down at me.

"Maggie, I think we should talk to your father."

"Last night, El, I did talk to him. It was a waste of time, honest. I hardly recognize him anymore."

"Maybe you could put it to him another way."

"You mean, tell him outright to change his platform, to come out with a slogan, Higher Taxes and Less Complaining?"

"No," she laughed. "But if we told him about Doreen, he'd listen, wouldn't he?"

"That's what I tried last night. Which didn't work."

"We've got to think, Mag. Hard."

I sat there, my chin cupped in my hand, thinking hard. For a few seconds my mind was a blank, and then I looked up at her and grabbed her leg. "El, if they have enough money for just one program, maybe we could sacrifice ours. Maybe they'd keep only the programs for the handicapped."

"Hey, Mag," she said with a tone of respect, "that's super. Let's ask him now."

"Well, no, I think I should sound out my mother, first." I looked at my watch. "She may be through with her committee by the time I get home."

Eloise agreed, and we decided it might be better if I approached Mom alone; you never know what mood they'll be in and even though Eloise is like family, you still can't depend on that one hundred percent if everything didn't fit into the right grooves during the day.

Besides, Eloise needed to take a shower.

Two cars were pulling out of our driveway and one from in front of the house, so I knew the meeting was over. I ran up the front steps and unlocked the door.

"Mom, I've got them! Come see!" Tommy's effervescence came in waves from the kitchen.

My mother was already halfway there, bubbling along with him. "Oh, the shirts, Tommy. Wonderful!"

In the hall there was still this subtle excitement in the air left over from the ladies who had just left. I wondered if this was the appropriate moment for what I was going to bring up. Maybe I should wait. There's supposed to be an exact right time for everything to happen in the world. I mean, I've heard that careers were made by doing or not doing something at a particular second. Maybe the angle of the earth wasn't in the perfect position with the orbit of the moon right now. I'm not an everyday follower of my astrology chart like Debbie, but it might be a good idea if I checked out the morning paper.

But even if the stars were correctly placed, this still wouldn't be the right time to talk to Mom. Not now, when she was carried away with enthusiasm for the Hal Thayer red, white, and blue T-shirts.

Yeah, I'll wait. I'll put my books away and then go in the kitchen, bright, cheery, and helpful. "Is there anything I can help you with, Mom, after I set the table?" I'll say.

That satisfied me, and I headed for my room. As I passed the stairs leading to the family room, I smelled something funny. I ran down, scared. When I got there I kept sniffing and making quick eye movements all around the room, looking for flames or at least smoke. There, on the aluminum extension table was a smoldering cigarette in our pewter nut dish. That's the one my mother likes best of all of what she calls her treasures.

Nobody in our family smokes, and not one of my parents' friends who I could think of did either. Obviously it was a committee person, which proved that my mother would put up with anything, even to ruining her favorite pewter dish and risk getting our house burned down, to have help in getting Daddy elected. I emptied the butt into the toilet and flushed it down.

That did it. I wasn't in a peaceful enough mood anymore to bring up anything so critical as the program for the handicapped.

As I left the john and passed the family room again, I noticed piles of stuff on the table that I hadn't paid attention to before. It looked like the brochures, posters, and bumper stickers which I hadn't seen yet. So I walked over. When I read them, I nearly dropped my mother's treasure on the floor.

BASICS ARE BEAUTIFUL—OUT WITH FRILLS

GOOD EDUCATION—NO NONSENSE

SPEND LESS, GET MORE FOR OUR TAX DOLLARS

All these terrible statements, one after the other in big print and bright colors.

Never, he would *never* agree to spend one extra cent of taxpayers' money, even for ketchup in the lunchroom, let alone for programs for the handicapped. I could just picture it: Ketchup on French Fries Will *Not Be Tolerated!* Money for signs like that in the cafeteria would be the only expense he would consider.

I slowly went upstairs, thinking it was hopeless. What, actually, could kids do to make their side known, or better, what kind of influence could they muster that would have any effect on the adult voters? I answered myself: nothing to the first question; nothing to the second.

The upstairs phone rang as I got there. My mother took it before the second ring. Naturally. Not a moment should be lost where she could further the cause.

"She's not home yet, Eloise," I heard her say.

"Yes, I am, Mom," I yelled down. "I just came in."

"Oh, she just came in, Eloise."

"I've got it, Mom," I called to her as I lifted the receiver.

"Okay."

I waited until I heard the click. My hello to Eloise was a groan, followed by "Forget it. You wouldn't believe."

"Maggie, wait'll you hear! Debbie called me, and I told her what you have in mind, and she came up with the idea of the century!"

I hadn't heard that kind of excitement in her voice since the baseball playoffs last June.

But I also knew that nothing anybody could

dream up would help. It had gone too far. So I asked her in a dull voice, "About what?"

"About our plan of action, you dodo!"

"El, if you're talking about the handi-capped—there isn't going to be any action. My father wouldn't even listen to us, no matter what we said or how we said it."

"We don't need his approval, Maggie. This is something we'll do on our *own!* Debbie is going to call up some kids; you and I will call more. We'll get the whole eighth grade, at least, behind us and *wow!*"

The more pepped up she was the more I got a sinking feeling without even knowing what the plan was. I knew there was no hope and that was that.

"So answer me. Say something, Maggie!"

"Okay, what's the plan?" There wasn't too much life to my tone.

"Maggie, what we are going to do," she began, carefully saying each word, and then pausing for the big one, "is *picket!*"

I repeated "Picket?" as if it was a new word in my vocabulary.

"Yah—picket, protest, *demonstrate!*"

"Demonstrate?" I repeated that, too, but unsteadily, as if I were in a rocky boat and losing my balance. "Against whom?"

"Against the school committee and any can-didates who shall be nameless who are for cutting programs. We're out to influence voters."

"Wh-where?" Could she mean in front of my father's store? Or our house?

"Lots of places. Like City Hall, the school

administration building, in front of all the schools, and especially in front of Woodrow Wilson!" She sounded as thrilled as if she'd been reinstated on the soccer team. "Well, aren't you impressed?"

"El," I said uncertainly, "against my own father—I don't know. . . ."

"But we'll all be doing it. And we won't use his name on our signs. We'll just tell it like it is."

"I don't—know . . . I mean, I'm not sure. I . . ."

"What are you afraid of, Maggie?"

"Well, it's not right. My parents—you know. . . ."

"But, Mag, you want to save the program for Doreen, don't you?"

"Of course."

"And saving the handicapped program was your idea in the first place, wasn't it?"

"Yes."

"Then, Mag, you'll do it. It's the only way!"

Chapter Fourteen

Saturday morning before I even got out of bed, Robby knocked on my door. What he does isn't precisely a knock; it's more of a punch with the side of his fist.

"Eloise is on the phone."

She was going to keep trying to convince me. I did and I didn't want to be convinced.

"What's the rush, El," I said sleepily into the phone. "You woke me up."

She wasn't wasting any time. "Debbie and Gail are coming over in half an hour. Hurry up with breakfast or come over here and eat it. We have a lot of work to do."

"I'll eat here. I'm not sure I'm interested in your 'work.' "

"Don't stall, Maggie. See you in fifteen minutes." She hung up.

That girl could be an asset to the armed forces in time of war.

Debbie and Gail were already there when I arrived.

"Maggie, you should organize it."

"Me? I haven't accepted the deal yet, and what do I know about organizing?"

"You've been watching what your parents have been doing. You ought to be an expert by now."

I had a sinking feeling, which must have shown on my face.

"We'll help, Maggie."

Oh, boy, if it weren't for Doreen . . .

So I went along with it. We formed a committee, they made me chairman, and all of a fast sudden I was number one in command. All day Saturday, Saturday night, Sunday, and Sunday night we worked and I organized. I made a schedule for times and places for discussion about plans. I appointed signmakers and a telephone squad. I had every kid in the eighth grade called on the phone excluding of course the seventeen handicapped kids at Woodrow Wilson. We wanted to keep it a secret from them.

By Monday the idea had snowballed. The eighth graders began telling their friends or relatives in the seventh and ninth grades, and offers for volunteers were made by the ton. In the lunchroom, in the hallways, between periods, and after school we met in little groups like conspirators—which we were.

· "I'm good at printing signs."

"I think we should wear black arm bands as a symbol of what the handicapped students might *lose.*"

"I'll make the arm bands."

"Should we get the teachers in on it?"

"*No!*"

"Why not?"

"My mother will find out in the school office!" I panicked. "Besides the teachers might object. Let's keep it going the way it is."

It was after C Block, two periods to go, and I was on my way to science.

"Hey, Maggie, wait up."

I knew the voice. I'd have waited forever. Stevie was behind me. It was the first time he'd ever called to me.

"What's this I've been hearing about you organizing a protest?"

I told him the general idea and that we were going to have a meeting after school to plan more details.

"How does your dad feel about what you're doing?"

"I haven't told him."

He laughed out loud and then whistled. The kind of whistle that says, You're in big trouble. Then the bell rang for the period to start.

"Let me hear how you're progressing," he said as we separated. "And if there's anything I can do."

Like visit me in the orphanage when my parents disown me.

"Maggie," one of the boys in my science class said in an undertone as I walked in there, "I don't think Barney Savage knew we weren't supposed to let the handicapped kids in on our plan."

That was all I needed. "Who'd he tell?"

"Nobody yet, but somebody better get to him before he spills it."

"Okay, I'll talk to him."

I didn't want to depend on anyone else to take care of it. I had to be sure he got the message.

[121]

The handicapped people better not find out, I thought. I wondered if Doreen had got wind of it. I'd find out, subtly, when I read to her the next day.

After the last period I saw Barney and straightened him out on keeping his mouth shut.

"Barney, we can't be too careful."

"Don't worry, Maggie. Now that I know."

"Did you let it slip to anyone?"

"No. No way."

Barney is not a person I would normally trust with any confidential material. He was the type who'd be tempted to tell just because I was putting so much importance on doing the opposite. But I didn't have much choice in this situation. We were accepting anyone who wanted to join up.

Back in my homeroom I took inventory of the contents of my desk. I reached in and pulled out some of the junk. There was a note from Gail, who had passed it to me in French last week; it said in English, "If I go to private school, do you think you could go, too?"

Yah. Fat chance, on my father's income. Anyhow I wouldn't want to leave W. W. as long as Stevie was there. I had another year before he'd be at high school, and now I could still bump into him in the corridors.

"Maggie, would you come here a minute, please?"

Miss Randall's tone didn't sound threatening, but we were all pretty shaky about teachers finding out about the protest. If she had, then of course I, being ringleader, would get charged with everything. I'd get expelled—dandy. Thrown out of school and into the orphanage in one fast swoop.

I inched over to her desk.

"I don't know if you'll be glad to hear this or not," she said, still without any clue in her voice or eyes. But I was ready for the worst. I kept a steady gaze on her.

"We received Doreen's history book in Braille this afternoon. It was completed before we expected it. So you won't need to read to her anymore."

I *do* need to read to her. I thought I was supposed to help her for the whole year. They get you all excited about something, and then they take it away. How can they do these things?

"I can see that you're disappointed, Maggie." She gave me a sunshiny smile. "I'm glad you feel that way. It shows you're concerned. But you know, there are other ways you can help her: being her friend is very important."

I believed that, but what was *she* leading up to? She must know about our plan, and she's about to warn me that it wouldn't help Doreen or the others. I forced out a smile.

Miss Randall kept talking. "Doreen has told me how much she enjoys being with you. I think you can be a real asset at the tutor-aide meeting on Thursday."

She paused, and I guess I was supposed to tell her I was flattered and thank her a million times. I knew very well that Thursday afternoon, the same as every afternoon until our demonstrations were over, I'd be very tied up planning for it.

I hesitated, and then what came out of my mouth was, "I—I may have to go to the dentist Thursday."

For the tenth time since my mother started working for the school, her job was in jeopardy because of her daughter's insubordination. Well, that's the way it was, that's all.

Miss Randall's sunshiny smile was clouded over. Maybe she saw through me. "When you find out, let me know, Maggie."

Sure.

I didn't bother cleaning out the rest of my desk. For all I cared there could be some moldy banana skins in there. The bell rang, which left me no time for it anyway.

That night was the usual up-down-answer-the-phone campaign routine. Then Mom said, "Honey, it's Doreen on the phone. Please try to make it short."

"Okay, Mom."

"Hi, Doreen."

"Maggie, did Miss Randall tell you?" She sounded the way I had felt when I found out she wouldn't need me to read to her.

But I couldn't be positive that that was her reaction. She might be thrilled to have more independence. So I was cautious in my answer.

"Yes . . . that'll be a big help to you, won't it?"

"Yes, but then we don't see each other!"

"Sure we will," I said with conviction.

"Oh, Maggie, I'm so glad. Could you come home with me tomorrow after school?"

Tomorrow after school we'll be having a meeting at Eloise's. "I can't tomorrow, Doreen."

"Wednesday I'm staying for piano. Can you come Thursday?"

I already told Miss Randall I might be at the dentist's on Thursday. I wasn't going to lie again. "I—I'm not sure, Doreen."

If only I could tell her. But I couldn't talk to her about it. Could I say, "Doreen we're the non-handicapped kids, and we are going to take care of things for you"? Nnh-nh.

She was disapponted.

I had to restrain myself from speaking out. "Maybe next week, Doreen." I knew that was unlikely, so I added, "You know, my folks are real busy with—uh—getting my father elected, and I might get stuck with my little brother after school." I hoped she'd buy that.

"After the election, things will be better," I added hopefully.

She didn't answer. Was she sorry she had been so frank with me so that now I thought she was stupid like everyone else did?

Mom was beside me making hurry-off-the-phone signs, so I had an excuse to say good-bye. Even though what I was planning was for Doreen's good, I didn't have too clean a feeling about being sneaky.

Our committee consisted of me, Eloise, Debbie, Gail, and a couple of eighth grade boys we appointed, since we didn't want to be accused of sexism. We were going to list all the stuff that people had volunteered for and size it up. All six of us were sitting on the front steps of the school building trying to make a decision where to meet. Debbie's house seemed like the safest place because her mother didn't get home from work until five-thirty, but it didn't give us all the time we wanted. Gail's mother did mostly hospital volunteer work, so we couldn't depend on her hours, and Eloise's mother had a part-time job that did not include Mondays. And me, of course, my house was out for obvious reasons.

"Dave, what's the scoop at your house? Will anybody be home?"

"My father's a dentist. His office is an extension of the garage."

"Forget it. Al, what does your father do?"

"He's an accountant, and his office is downtown. It's my mother you have to watch out for."

"Great. What's her thing?"

"She paints."

"So?"

"Her studio is on the premises."

Eloise groaned. "I can see we made a big mistake choosing you guys to be on our committee."

"Well, was one of the requirements to have an empty house?"

"It should have been."

We settled for Debbie's and decided to work fast and get out of there before her mother came home.

"When is our first march?" Al asked when we opened up the meeting.

"Maggie, you've got that information."

I pulled the vital-statistics notebook out of my purse. "October twenty-first. Two weeks before voting day."

"When is the next one?"

"We haven't planned it yet."

"Well, I think," Al said as if he had great respect for his opinion, "that we should have several. You know, like bomb them."

"Several?"

"If we're going to influence the voters, a lot of action will make a big impact," Al said flatly.

"Like how many?" Debbie challenged him.

"Like five marches, one day after the other."

"Five!"

"How many kids are marching?" Dave asked.

I consulted my notebook again. "One hundred and twenty."

There was absolute silence as the significance of that number of kids marching for five consecutive days must have struck every one of us. So I did some thinking. "Wait a minute, everybody. If we want this election to come out the way we want it to, we're going to have to do it *right*. We'll lose the whole effect if we stage too many marches. Two are enough. The first one should be about ten days before election, and they'll never expect another. Then the day before voting we'll surprise them, and that will bring the best result. As long as we all know what our goal is, we can't lose!" I said all that as if I were an orator on a soapbox.

It was like firecrackers had exploded.

"Right on, Maggie!"

"You bet. We can do it!"

"We'll show 'em!"

Eloise gave me a very approving look. "We knew who to pick for chairman, Maggie, didn't we?"

I grinned at her. Maybe they did. Yup—maybe so.

Chapter Fifteen

The next two weeks were crammed. We needed representatives from the seventh and ninth grades, which would also give us more houses to alternate our meetings in.

"Who do you want from the ninth?" Eloise asked me privately. I had told her about my two conversations in the hall with Stevie, and she thought I should call him. "He did say if there was anything he could do, Mag."

"Yes, but—oh I don't know."

"Call him."

I did.

"Is—is S-Stevie there?" I stuttered into the phone. It was probably his mother who answered, and if there's one thing I know mothers of boys hate, it's girls calling their sons—chasing them.

"This is Maggie," I half whispered when he came to the phone.

"Oh, hi, Maggie." His voice sounded like music, and I could picture his handsome face.

"Since you offered, Stevie, I thought I'd ask. Can you be a ninth grade representative for our demonstration?"

I'll give him this much—at least he thought about it for a second before he gave me his answer: Gee, he was real sorry but he couldn't. He had rehearsals, and he was on the school paper this year. He'd march, though. I could depend on him for that.

I wanted to ask him, Suppose a rehearsal is scheduled. Will that make a difference where you'll go that day? I mean, I happened to know that Carrie Dean got the part of Rebecca as well as understudy for Emily.

What I said was "Oh, that's too bad, Stevie."

I took it as a personal rebuff, but Eloise said I shouldn't harbor any such feelings. A person has just so many hours in the day, and his were already filled.

"Okay, Eloise, but just the same, I'm harboring."

Also, it didn't help when I saw Carrie and a table full of actors from *Our Town* all sitting together in the lunchroom. Unfortunately Debbie and Gail were already sitting at a table near the back, which meant I had to overhear a bunch of terrific laughing as I passed them, and one voice saying, "And let's not forget the cast party, kids. It's going to be even better than last year."

That hurt, I'm telling you. The only saving grace was that Stevie didn't happen to be there at the time.

We got somebody else for a ninth grade representative, and we also added eight more to our telephone-caller list. Things were getting more hectic with each day, and we were as nervous about leaks as if we were working on classified information at the Pentagon.

"Where do we meet today?"

That question would come up during lunch, and we'd be so intent on our plans that we didn't even know how punk the food was.

"It's Tuesday, so that means Eloise's. Her mother won't be home until late."

"Tell the kids who want to submit posters today, that's where we'll be."

The word was passed that as many arm bands would be worn and as many banners would be carried as could go around. The whole committee had to judge every poster that was submitted, and we had to reject some, like Give the Handicapped a Break.

The ones we chose were:

PROGRAMS FOR THE HANDICAPPED ARE A MUST

HANDICAPPED STUDENTS HAVE RIGHTS—
DON'T DENY THEM

SCHOOL COMMITTEE PLEASE TAKE NOTE:
KEEP THE HANDICAPPED EDUCATED

Actually I wasn't too thrilled about using that word, "handicapped," but Al said that was exactly the idea we wanted to call people's attention to. The rest of the committee agreed, so I went along with it.

My biggest fear through all this was that my parents would find out. I mean, no matter how much I disagreed with my father and no matter how sincere my own convictions were, I didn't want to hurt my parents. I felt that even stronger, I think, than getting in trouble with them. But there was no turning back. I was in this for Doreen and people like her, and I was determined to see it through.

It finally got to be October twenty-second, the day before countdown. I think we were more on edge that day than at any time leading up to it. It was like before a term exam. We rehearsed all our signals, checked and rechecked with everyone about everything, and were reasonably satisfied that we were coordinated and in sync.

"Remember," we reminded our representatives, "when the last bell rings tomorrow, no one is supposed to jump up or behave in any way to cause suspicion."

"Okay, we've got it."

"We will take our books as usual and normally walk to the door and *normally* proceed to City Hall."

"Got it. Got it."

"And no one will put on arm bands or hold up banners until we are out of sight of the school building."

"Check."

"When we get to City Hall we will form a circle as best we can and keep marching around in an orderly fashion."

"Got it."

"*Orderly.* You get *that?*"

"Got it."

Then the Day arrived. We had planned no little meetings in the lunchroom, no code words to be passed in the corridors that said one thing but meant something different in case a teacher was in hearing distance. We all managed to get through our class sessions without anyone fainting or screaming from anxiety.

The last bell had rung, and no one was even supposed to look at the clock. We deliberately stayed put, and then, as casually as possible, we gathered our books, stood, and walked out. Normally.

About five of us from the committee were waiting for Debbie. We were getting really tense because she was two minutes late. Then we saw her coming out the door, looking ashen.

"What's up?" We held our breath.

"We goofed," she said hoarsely.

Not one of us could get the courage to ask why.

"I just heard this minute," she went on in a hushed voice, "that we have to have a permit to march."

"Permit? So what does that mean?"

"I don't know, but it's . . . well, it's something we're supposed to *have*."

"So what happens if we don't?"

"I don't know."

"Who cares?"

"Let's go already!"

"Yes, but what will happen when they find out we're illegal?" Debbie couldn't accept our unexpected fearlessness.

"It's too late to go back now, Deb," I pointed out. "Step on it."

"They won't put us in jail; don't worry." Eloise tried to be reassuring. "So let's go!"

Everyone outside the school started walking in the same direction at the same time. There was no way around that, since our objective was only to get to City Hall. I began hurrying.

"Maggie, you're walking too fast. We're sure to attract attention." Dave put a restraining hand on my sleeve.

"That's exactly what we want to attract," I told him. "At this point in time, Dave, we're red hot." I could feel excitement absolutely swelling inside me. "At this point in time," I repeated, my voice getting stronger with confidence, "we can run if we want to."

"Yeah," he said as if awed by my authority.

City Hall is six blocks from school, and with each block we kept gaining momentum. Everybody must have felt the same impulse, because by the time we were at the four-way intersection leading to the square where the building is set back on a huge lawn, hordes of the kids were there. The six of us were first at the curb, and when I turned around and saw the size of the mob behind me, I suddenly felt like I was leading an army.

"Okay, everybody," I called out facing them. "When the light turns green we all march across and keep going even when the light turns red. We don't stop until we have all congregated in a body in front of the steps to the front door."

I scanned the group. They were four across on the sidewalk and a block deep, with some stragglers picking up speed behind them. "Can you all hear me?" I called out louder.

"Yes," they shouted back in unison.

There wasn't a familiar face—only one unrecognizable mass. It didn't matter. We all had the same mission, and who they were made no difference. Then I saw an arm waving higher than anyone's head. A voice called out, "We keep going until we're all in front of the steps. Right, Maggie?" It was Stevie. He came!

"Right on!" I yelled back. I turned and addressed my committee. "Are you with me?"

"Yes!"

Then, without a word, everyone's eyes were on the lights. If we'd had some microphone gadget attached to our hearts I bet it would have sounded like bombs ticking, ready to go off. The light turned green. We moved. The light changed to red, and we kept moving. The cars, stopped in traffic, didn't even honk, waiting patiently for that multitude to clear the street.

Between the lawn and the City Hall steps is a curved driveway bordered by a broad sidewalk. The pedestrian section was big enough for us to spread out and make two big circles, one inside the other. It took a little time to arrange ourselves and hold up our banners. Eloise, Gail, and I were on the outside; Debbie, Al, and Dave were on the inside.

"Should we chant something?" one of the boys asked me.

We hadn't thought of that.

"Why not?" Eloise was charged up.

"How about We're Marching for the Handicapped?" Al suggested. I squirmed thinking of how that might affect them. "No. How about, We're Marching for Our Special Friends?" I said.

"Super."

"Okay, let's say it in rhythm, with accents on *march* and *special*."

A few of us tried it out a couple of times, and I thought of another line that went in the same rhythm: Let's *Keep* Them in Our *School*. Two more times we rehearsed it loud enough for the rest of the marchers to hear. I told them I'd give the signal when to start and when to stop, since we didn't want to chant continuously. We all took a deep breath, and we were ready.

I raised my hand, then cut the air with it for the starting signal. We circled and we chanted:

We're Marching for Our Special Friends
Let's Keep Them in Our School.

We're Marching for Our Special Friends
Let's Keep Them in Our School.

A few people stopped on their way to or from the city hall; they seemed interested in what we were doing.

"What are they saying?" I heard one of them ask the lady she was with.

"Who knows? These kids today, they protest everything."

They walked on, but I felt like telling her angrily that all she had to do was read our signs and she'd find out what was going on in Oakdale. She was the kind who probably wanted no taxes and all the services. At least my father didn't want something for nothing.

We kept chanting as we circled around. I wasn't going to have them stop until those two ladies were out of sight.

At this point, what with the chanting and the size of the group, it must have seemed like a disturbance, and besides people stopping, others were looking out their windows.

"How we doing?" Gail had this expression like she was having a ball.

"So far so good," Eloise said. "But it would be better if more voters saw us."

"Here's one coming at us right now," I said with a queasy feeling in my stomach.

"Where?"

"That man in the blue uniform, otherwise known as a policeman."

"Oh-oh. Debbie was right," Gail moaned.

"Not necessarily," Eloise said. "I've been thinking that if you're under eighteen you don't need a permit to march. I mean, what can they do to you?"

"Stick you in prison," Gail answered.

The policeman stopped in front of a girl about five feet away from us.

"Hold it, hold it," he said, raising his arm.

She had a panicky look and turned toward me.

"You have permission to be here?" he asked her, not too friendly.

"Ohmigod," I heard Debbie say behind us. "My mother will send me to Florida for sure when she finds out what I've done."

"You should only be so lucky to get sent to Florida instead of the slammer," Gail said between her clenched teeth.

By this time the chanting had quieted down, and the march had come to a full stop. I turned to face the kids behind me and gave the signal to quit chanting. When I faced front again, I noticed the girl the policeman had spoken to was pointing at me. Yeah, that's what I thought would happen.

"Who's your ringleader?" he must have asked her, and she ratted.

As he came toward me, he looked nine feet tall and half a ton in weight. I expected him to reach for his pistol, but he just glowered at me and repeated the question he'd asked the other girl, only this time it was more a demand.

"You have permission to be here?"

"Sure," I heard myself say while Gail groaned and Eloise made some kind of agonized sound.

He looked at me, very uncertain of my credentials while he seemed to be waiting for me to produce the permit. Since I was stalling anyway, I thought I'd wait until he actually put it in words, so I just gave him my most innocent, honest expression.

"You see, little girl," he said insultingly, "I wasn't informed there was to be any demonstrations here today."

"Oh, well, in that case," I started frantically looking in my purse. "I was sure I had it here," I said, shoving everything around. I looked over at Eloise, "Do you have it, El?"

"I'll look," she said accommodatingly and started searching in her shoulder bag.

"Maggie!" Gail let out a scream.

"What's the matter?"

"Look over at the parking lot!"

We looked. Three specially built vans and two station wagons were lined up, and the five drivers, one of them Doreen's mother, were in the process of opening doors and hatches. As we watched, wheelchairs with people in them rolled down the ramps of the vans, and kids with those metal walkers were getting out of the station wagons. We kept our eyes on the scene as if they were held by magnets, and we watched, speechless. A boy in one of those motorized chairs wheeled himself near the edge of the lot nearest where we were and stopped. With his back to us he began giving orders to the rest of those kids, moving his arms and pointing, like he was telling them where to place themselves.

"There's Joey!" Eloise shouted as if he'd been found after a year's disappearance.

I saw him getting out of the car with about four or five other handicapped people I recognized. There were also some in the group I had never seen before.

"Doreen!" I spotted her standing right in front of the boy who seemed to be their leader. He was yelling, and she was listening.

"What are they doing?"

"What's going on?"

Confusion and questions were coming from all directions.

"Hey, that's Johnny Rossman," a voice from back of our group called out.

Oh, so that's who that boy is in the wheelchair. The one Doreen said could shoot baskets as good as Danny Cavelletti. What *was* going on? Were they going to have a wheelathon to advertise the basketball Olympics?

Four boys were holding something attached to two long poles. Johnny looked as though he was giving them orders. Then two of them, holding one of the poles, started walking and stopped when they got about ten yards away from us. As they walked it looked like they were unwinding a scroll that was connected to the pole the two boys at the other end were holding. When it was completely unwound, we were able to see what was written on it:

WE'RE ALL IN THIS TOGETHER

PROGRAMS ARE FOR EVERYONE

WE DON'T WANT IT IF EVERYONE CAN'T HAVE IT

Then the whole parking lot exploded with vibrations. Everyone out there recited, way stronger than a chant, what was printed on the signs. Other kids were raising banners and kept repeating whatever was written on them with more intensity each time it was their turn:

WE BELIEVE IN EQUALITY

EQUAL RIGHTS FOR ALL

It wasn't over yet. Johnny was almost standing up with excitement. "And now"—he was acting like he was conducting a choir as he pointed to two other boys—"the last one."

The two he pointed at weren't particularly tall, and one was even sitting in his wheelchair. He had his poster rolled up on his lap, and he wheeled himself over beside Johnny. Doreen, who was still standing there, reached out for one end of the pole, and they both started unwinding it until it was completely open. Then, when they held it out in front of them, we saw what it said:

WE LEARN TOGETHER OR NOT AT ALL

Then they spoke it like it was a poem or a psalm they believed in. Their voices resounded through the whole lawn, pavement, and parking lot as if they were a thousand voices strong.

One small group of handicapped kids had stolen the show from a hundred and twenty able-bodied ones in nothing flat.

Chapter Sixteen

OAKDALE STUDENTS STAGE RALLY

That was the headline of a story on page three in the *Weekly Tribune* the next morning. The article went on:

Well over 100 Oakdale Junior High School youngsters gathered in front of City Hall yesterday afternoon to protest the threat of elimination of extracurricular activities.

In a heart-warming act of self-sacrifice, seventh, eighth, and ninth graders carried placards demanding that courses for the physically handicapped not be scrapped if proposed tax cuts are passed.

Margaret [Maggie] Thayer, eighth grade student at Woodrow Wilson and chairman of the protest, praised her committee, composed of Gail Sheppard, Debbie Reinhall, Eloise Barton, Albert Philbrick, and Dave Evans, but Maggie herself modestly remained in the background. She is the daughter of Hal Thayer, candidate for the school committee and one of the tax-cut supporters. Maggie stated positively her father was unaware of the demonstration and had no part in anything connected with it.

In a surprise move, seventeen physically handicapped students put on a simultaneous protest pleading for continuation of the programs, not for themselves, but for all students in the school system.

Who says there's anything wrong with kids nowadays?

"Surprise move" was an understatement. We were stupefied by those kids in the parking lot. As soon as they got through with their chanting, it seemed as if everyone in the state suddenly fell from the sky onto City Hall property. It was like armies moved in, talking, pushing, and shoving. Then I saw this guy coming toward me.

"Officer Hayes here tells me you're the young lady responsible for this demonstration. What's your name?"

I was too awed and too scared I was going to get arrested to answer right off. The first thing I thought of was that he should read me my rights.

"I'm Carl Fisher, a reporter with the *Weekly Tribune*," he introduced himself and showed me his I.D.

I looked at it, but my head was in such a muddle that I still thought he was a plainclothes detective.

"What are you going to put in the paper about us?" Debbie asked him anxiously.

"I have to get the facts first, and then I'll know." He gave her a professional smile. "Now, what's your name?" he repeated his question to me.

"Maggie—Margaret Thay—" I clamped my mouth shut. If he knew my name, he would get my father in trouble. Nobody would vote for him. Oh-darn-oh-rats-oh-*damn!* That's what I wanted, wasn't it?

"How do you spell your last name, Maggie?" I heard him, and I knew he was determined to get his story. So I spelled it.

Then about ten other kids wanted to get their names in the paper, but my buddies said if any credit was being given, let the right ones get it. I didn't give any details; my committee told it all. A couple of clods from my class added the information about my father. If he never got mad in his life before, he'd blow his top now.

"My own daughter disgracing me by a public display!" he'd roar. "Protesting against your father's principles," he'd bellow.

My father wasn't the roar-and-bellow type but what I did was going to make him a changed man.

And my mother—I could hear her. She's no roarer or bellower either, but I could hear her all right. "Margaret," she'd start, "you know what this means to my job. The school department will sever their connection with me immediately and for life."

I was ready to cry, visualizing the sadness in my mother's face.

"And to do this behind our backs," they'd both say, and wag their heads.

All I wanted right then was a miracle. Any kind, just so's my parents would forgive me and those seventeen kids would get their programs.

That's when I heard Doreen's voice but couldn't locate her in the crowd. "Maggie! Maggie!"

"Doreen, I'm over here," I yelled, knowing she would follow the direction of the sound.

I kept thinking how wonderful all those kids in the parking lot were, but I knew the power of politicians. Doreen would never get her program. She'd never play the piano. My parents would think I was a troublemaker, and she'd be sent back to her boarding school for the blind, and no one with sight would ever get to know her.

"Doreen!" I jammed my way through the crowd using my whole body as a ramrod.

Last fall when I saw Stevie standing at the other side of the gym from where I was, I couldn't get to him fast enough. But this rush to get through wasn't the same at all. With Stevie, what I wanted then was to look at him and get a thrill out of it. With Doreen now, it wasn't that *I* had to feel good—it was her. I had to tell her what I thought of what she did—what we all thought. The trouble those handicapped kids must have had arranging their demonstration, making those signs, getting in and out of those cars. I mean we thought it was tricky enough working undercover and trying to keep everything quiet, but it must have been ten times harder for them. How did they . . . *Say,* how did they know what we were doing, anyhow?

"Maggie!"

There she was. She had wedged her way

through the mob and had her arms outstretched. I held her hard, and neither of us said a word. When we drew apart, both of us started to speak at the same time and then laughed out loud.

"How did you know what we were planning?" I asked her.

"Actually we didn't know until last week. Someone in Mr. Kahn's room spilled the beans about you."

"Barney Savage!"

"Yes, that's his name," she nodded, remembering.

"I knew I couldn't trust that kid!"

"But Maggie," she said, surprised, "if he hadn't said anything we never would have found out, and we couldn't have done this. And when we did find out, we wanted to do it on our own— the same as you wanted to."

I felt like a crumb. Why was I so sure only us kids could handle a problem? It never crossed our minds that they would feel that way, work on it, or carry it out. Worst of all, we thought of them as helpless. Boy, if anyone was handicapped, it was us—in our brains.

There were a lot of police giving orders by then, trying to get the crowd to move. As organized as we were at the beginning, it was a disorganized gang breaking up. Doreen and I got separated, and I couldn't even find Eloise or anyone I knew real well to walk home with.

Mom was in the family room with a meeting when I got in. Robby was playing with a friend in the back yard, and Tommy was working on a bike in the garage. That meant three members of my family were probably unaware of the disaster . . . so far.

It got to be six o'clock, and Mom's ladies had just left, and Daddy wasn't home yet. That was a bad sign. Where was he so late? Answering questions about me down at police headquarters? At City Hall, resigning his candidacy out of shame? At the principal's office signing papers to withdraw me from Woodrow Wilson?

Ring!

I jumped. And then I ran to the phone before my mother would get the news.

"H-h-h-hello."

"Hi, sweetheart."

"Daddy?" I asked hesitantly. I knew his voice, but I didn't expect he'd still be calling me sweetheart.

"Any other man call you sweetheart, Maggie?" He said it lightly.

I swallowed and took a chance. "Not yet, Dad."

"Glad to hear that. Had a good day, honey?"

Was he serious? Was he trapping me? Should I confess? I took a deep breath. "Fine, Daddy."

"Good. Put your mother on."

I handed her the phone, still doubtful about how much he knew. I left the room. I didn't have the intestinal fortitude to listen. A couple of minutes later Mom called me. I went back to the kitchen, my stomach churning and the rest of me palpitating.

"Maggie, Ken Berns wants all the committee people for a meeting tonight at his house."

Then my father knew. They were going to come out stronger for the cuts. He must have used big self-control with me on the phone.

"We're getting together as soon as possible, so Daddy called the deli to bring in sandwiches."

"Is—something wrong, Mom?"

"No, dear, but it's very close to election, and everyone happens to be free tonight, so it seemed like a good time to review our position on all the issues."

She didn't suspect anything.

"Mom, do you—I mean, do you think there'll be any changes."

"Daddy still feels the same, Maggie. He's determined to satisfy the needs of the parents and the children to the best of his ability."

That said it all. It meant he'd stick to his guns, but at least he didn't know about his daughter's performance that afternoon. Actually, it was a break for me they were having the meeting: I wouldn't have to face my father tonight. All I did was nod and hope I looked like I at least understood, if I didn't agree.

"Maggie, you heat supper for the three of you, and Tommy will help you clean up. See that Robby gets to bed at his usual time. I don't think we'll be too late." She gave me her usual kiss. I knew I had won a temporary reprieve.

I was glad to see her go. I'd happily heat up supper, and I wouldn't care if Tommy didn't lift a finger in preparation or cleanup.

The next morning at a quarter to seven, I was the one who picked up the paper outside our front door. At the breakfast table my father was the one who turned to page three and read the article out loud.

Not even Tommy made a sound. Robby was completely preoccupied with getting his piece of bread to absorb all the egg yolk on his plate. I could feel Mom's eyes on me as Daddy read the last words. I hadn't taken my eyes off him from the first word he uttered. Then, the silence. Like we were waiting for the ax to fall.

"Daddy!" I couldn't wait another second. I shrieked his name and stood up. "Oh, Daddy, if you have to disown me I'll understand, but *please* don't campaign for cuts in the handicapped students' program. Those seventeen people need a lot of extras; they need the resource room and electives and sports. Daddy, you should see Johnny Rossman play basketball. He's even better than Danny Cavelletti. And Joey—Joey has done so much better since he's had speech therapy. Please, Daddy!" I couldn't mention Doreen and her piano lessons, because I knew if I did I'd bust out crying.

There wasn't a peep out of anyone when I got through. Robby quit sopping up his bread and stared, first at me and then at my father, in awe. Even Tommy still didn't have anything to say. Everyone waited.

My father folded the newspaper and put it on the table beside his silverware. "Come here, Maggie."

He didn't yell it or sound angry. He just said it quietly. But that's my father. He'd been hurt to the quick and couldn't raise his voice. If I had courage, real gutsy courage, I'd have killed myself right then and there. The most dangerous implement on the table was a butter knife and I knew, even without guts, that I couldn't get very far with that. I remembered Gail threatening to kill herself. I wondered what kind of knife she had planned on using.

I shoved back my chair and took the few steps to get over to him. I couldn't look at my mother and realized how weak I was. Not for not being able to look at her, but because I knew I must be a basically weak person. Being afraid is weak. I'd been afraid to get involved in the tutor-aide program. And that had to be the reason I didn't make the Dramatics Club—I was afraid to let myself get loose and be myself. Were other people like that, or was I like a different breed?

Daddy grabbed my arms. "Who said anything about disowning you?"

That meant he'd figure out some unspeakable punishment. I tried to swallow without making it sound like thunder.

"Maggie, I think you might like to know what happened at our meeting last night." He was looking deep into my eyes, and I tried not to blink.

I felt my mother's hand on my shoulder. I was like the middle of a sandwich and just as inanimate. I couldn't speak.

He was still holding on to my arms. "While you were working out your very commendable demonstration, we and our committee weren't ignoring the feelings and needs of all of you."

Commendable demonstration. That must have been sarcasm.

"Well, I—we—" I started to stammer a justification for what I had done, but he interrupted.

"We should have had more discussion, you and Mother and I. I am responsible for that lack, and I am sorry. You see, Maggie, we've been on the same side as you, but we've gone about finding a solution in a different way.

I couldn't answer him. No matter what the reporter wrote in the newspaper, my way wasn't right.

"Hey, what's this all about?" Tommy stood up, no longer able to stay quiet.

"Can I have some more milk, Mommy?" Robby reminded us he was still there.

"Let's all sit down, and we'll explain everything." Mom got busy pouring the milk as I went back to my chair, not sure of what most of it was about either.

Daddy presided, but he directed most of what he said to me. "Our friends, who are backing my campaign, have been very concerned, as your mother and I were, about how to resolve the problem of keeping good education for our community and at the same time lowering the tax rate that pays for it. But we never planned to do away with the program for the handicapped. We were working on the best way to *save* it."

Talk about rumors flying around.

Mom filled in some details. "Your father thought of the idea of consolidating schools. That would make it possible to keep all the programs for the handicapped as well as almost all for the rest of the students."

Tommy asked, "What's consolidating schools mean?"

"It means closing some schools and combining the rest of them. There has been a decrease in pupil population, and so we could combine two schools in one building without overcrowding anyone."

Then that meant Doreen and Joey and all of them could have their special needs taken care of and their electives, too!

"So we had discussions with the superintendent of schools as well as all the school principals and the aldermen. At last night's meeting we got their final approval on the consolidation issue." Daddy continued bringing us up-to-date with the facts.

"So you see, Maggie, if I'm elected, what you protested against won't happen anyway," he summed it up and then added, "but we're very proud of what you did, sweetheart."

"You bet we are," Mom echoed.

"Proud." My mouth was dry as I said the word. I shook my head, No. "You grownups worked it all out. No matter which way you look at it, what we kids did was a waste of time."

"Waste of time!" My mother, father, *and* Tommy let that out in a yell.

"What you did showed a very fine character, Maggie. Don't you ever forget it." My dad said that like he really did mean for me to remember it always.

"And courageous." Mom said that in absolutely velvet tones.

"Hey, Maggie, that took *guts!*" Tommy leaned over the table to make sure I heard every word.

I did. Every word.

Mom was looking at me. "How would you like to go to Oakdale High next year, Maggie?"

I knew I was nowhere near the top ten in my class, so I didn't think I was going to skip the ninth grade and get to be a sophomore next year. What was she getting at?

"I don't understand what you mean," I said.

"Because of Daddy's plan, the three junior highs will consolidate into one with only seventh and eighth grades, and Oakdale High will be a four-year school with ninth, tenth, eleventh, and twelfth." She said it matter-of-factly, but when the meaning landed in my skull I let out a shout.

"Does that mean you'd like it?"

"*Like* it? *Love* it! I've got to call Eloise."

"Finish your breakfast. You'll be going to school with her in ten minutes."

"Mom, I can't eat another mouthful. I'm too excited. I'll have a huge lunch, really I will." I got to the phone as the doorbell rang. Someone answered it, and before I got through dialing the number, I heard Eloise's voice.

"Hey, there's a funny connection here. Eloise is talking to me, and I didn't finish making the call."

"That's because Eloise is standing behind you," her voice said.

I turned around. "What are you doing here?" I asked stupidly.

"Making a house call, dummy. Hang up the phone."

I hung it up. "El, did you see the paper?"

She gave me a slow smile, widening to a full grin. "That's why I'm making this house call, kiddo. How did they take it?" She tossed her head in the direction of the dining room.

"Proud of me—of all of us." I said in amazement.

"My parents gave me the same treatment. Mag, do you think it will have any good effect? I mean, what about your father . . . ?"

For the moment I had forgotten the real reason I called her on the phone. "El!" I let out one holler. "El, you and I are going to Oakdale High next year because of my wonderful, marvelous father!"

Her face went blank. "Clue me in, Maggie."

I clued her and then we howled, we got silly, we danced around the room.

"Mag, do you realize what going to O.H. next year really means?"

"The list is endless." I looked at her dreamily. "Like you never know who you might bump into in the corridors."

"Not only bump into, Mag, but talk to. And you know how come that will happen?"

"Because we'll be going to O.H., dummy."

"No, another reason. Do you know what you finally have?"

"Hysterics?"

"No."

"Bad breath?"

"Be serious, Maggie."

"I give up."

"You, Ms. Thayer, finally got yourself some *pizzazz*." She beamed at me.

I had forgotten about that. I really didn't know if I had it or not, but I was grateful she said it. "So have you, El."

"Oh, I've always known that, kiddo."

"Girls, you'll be late for school." Mom walked into the hall. "Do you want to ride with me? Edith Connors is picking me up."

Eloise and I looked at each other and shook our heads.

"We'll walk. We want to meet the kids on the way."

Before we left, I went back to the dining room. Daddy was clearing the table. "Dad . . . "

He looked up at me and said over a stack of dishes, "Maggie, I could use some help these last days before the election. How about using your talents in my behalf?"

Like they say, that was the icing on the cake. The look I gave him he didn't need to wonder what my answer was.

"I would like people to go from house to house and drop off brochures," he explained. "If you and about three or four of your friends would cover the ward . . . "

He didn't have to finish talking either. I gave him a very big hug and thanked him again for the privilege.

My father won the election. I like to think my efforts did help. Mine and Eloise's and Debbie's and Gail's . . . and a couple of others'. I got a lot of offers when I mentioned to the gang of kids standing around my table at lunch that I needed people to hand out literature about my dad.

"That's one of my strong points." I knew Stevie's voice, of course.

"I'll give you a tryout," I said easily, eyeing him with a non-actressy look. "And one more person will be all we need."

It was just a coincidence that Danny Cavelletti was standing beside Eloise, and he volunteered, too, which made it nice and even. We decided to work in pairs, so it just happened that Eloise covered her streets with Danny, and Stevie and I teamed up for ours.

About a month after that, Doreen was in her first piano recital. My unbiased opinion is that she was the best one playing. It was held in the auditorium of Oakdale High. That was the first time I'd ever been in that building. It's huge. But it was cozy sitting beside Stevie, and afterward a bunch of us kids—including Doreen, her brother, and her parents—went to Bailey's for fabulous sundaes.

My relationship with Stevie is definitely improving. And I'm not minimizing that. But I found out it's not pizzazz that really matters— being natural helps a lot. And anyway, there's a more important thing than—well, trying to be an actress—that is the absolute, ultimate end.